Praise for
New York Times and *USA TODAY* bestselling author
Brenda Jackson

"Brenda Jackson writes romance that sizzles
and characters you fall in love with."
New York Times and *USA TODAY* bestselling author
Lori Foster

"Jackson's trademark ability to weave
multiple characters and side stories together
makes shocking truths all the more exciting."
—*Publishers Weekly*

"There is no getting away from the sex appeal and
charm of Jackson's Westmoreland family."
—*RT Book Reviews* on *Feeling the Heat*

"Jackson's characters are wonderful, strong,
colorful and hot enough to burn the pages."
—*RT Book Reviews* on *Westmoreland's Way*

"The kind of sizzling, heart-tugging story
Brenda Jackson is famous for."
—*RT Book Reviews* on *Spencer's Forbidden Passion*

"This is entertainment at its best."
—*RT Book Reviews* on *Star of His Heart*

* * *

The Real Thing is part of The Westmorelands series:
A family bound by loyalty...and love!
Only from *New York Times* bestselling author
Brenda Jackson and Harlequin Desire!

* * *

If you're on Twitter,
tell us what you think of Harlequin Desire!
#harlequindesire

P9-CCW-077

Dear Reader,

I can't believe I'm writing about one of those notorious Westmorelands—one of the last four in the Denver Series. When I first introduced the twins—Adrian and Aidan, Bailey and Bane—I understood the pain that motivated them to create havoc in their wake. And I knew by the time I wrote their stories they would have gotten older, improved their attitude and behavior. I also knew the person with which they chose to share their life would appreciate everything about them, and help any additional healing that was needed in their life.

I chose Trinity for Adrian Westmoreland because she was headstrong, independent. What she thought she wanted most out of life was a medical career and to live in a small town. It took Adrian Westmoreland to show her that all your wants and desires mean nothing unless you can share them with the person you truly love.

I hope you enjoy this story about Adrian and Trinity.

Happy Reading!

Brenda Jackson

BRENDA JACKSON

THE REAL THING

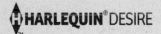

If you purchased this book without a cover you should be aware
that this book is stolen property. It was reported as "unsold and
destroyed" to the publisher, and neither the author nor the
publisher has received any payment for this "stripped book."

To the love of my life, Gerald Jackson, Sr.

To my readers
who continue to inspire me to reach higher heights.

To my family—
the Hawks, Streaters and Randolphs who continue to support me
in all my endeavors. I couldn't ask to be a part of a better family.

For we cannot but speak the things
which we have seen and heard.
—*Acts* 4:20 NKJV

ISBN-13: 978-0-373-73300-2

THE REAL THING

Copyright © 2014 by Brenda Streater Jackson

Recycling programs
for this product may
not exist in your area.

All rights reserved. Except for use in any review, the reproduction
or utilization of this work in whole or in part in any form by any
electronic, mechanical or other means, now known or hereafter
invented, including xerography, photocopying and recording, or in
any information storage or retrieval system, is forbidden without
the written permission of the publisher, Harlequin Enterprises Limited,
225 Duncan Mill Road, Don Mills, Ontario M3B 3K9, Canada.

This is a work of fiction. Names, characters, places and incidents are
either the product of the author's imagination or are used fictitiously, and
any resemblance to actual persons, living or dead, business establishments,
events or locales is entirely coincidental.

This edition published by arrangement with Harlequin Books S.A.

For questions and comments about the quality of this book, please contact us
at CustomerService@Harlequin.com.

® and TM are trademarks of Harlequin Enterprises Limited or its corporate
affiliates. Trademarks indicated with ® are registered in the United States Patent
and Trademark Office, the Canadian Trade Marks Office and in other countries.

H HARLEQUIN®
™ www.Harlequin.com

Printed in U.S.A.

Books by Brenda Jackson

Harlequin Desire

*A Wife for a Westmoreland #2077
*The Proposal #2089
*Feeling the Heat #2149
*Texas Wild #2185
*One Winter's Night #2197
*Zane #2239
*Canyon #2245
*Stern #2251
*The Real Thing #2287

Silhouette Desire

*Delaney's Desert Sheikh #1473
*A Little Dare #1533
*Thorn's Challenge #1552
*Stone Cold Surrender #1601
*Riding the Storm #1625
*Jared's Counterfeit Fiancée #1654
*The Chase Is On #1690
*The Durango Affair #1727
*Ian's Ultimate Gamble #1745
*Seduction, Westmoreland Style #1778
*Spencer's Forbidden Passion #1838
*Taming Clint Westmoreland #1850
*Cole's Red-Hot Pursuit #1874
*Quade's Babies #1911
*Tall, Dark...Westmoreland! #1928
*Westmoreland's Way #1975
*Hot Westmoreland Nights #2000
*What a Westmoreland Wants #2035

Harlequin Kimani Arabesque

ΔWhispered Promises
ΔEternally Yours
ΔOne Special Moment
ΔFire and Desire
ΔSecret Love
ΔTrue Love
ΛSurrender
ΔSensual Confessions
ΔInseparable
ΔCourting Justice

Harlequin Kimani Romance

ΩSolid Soul #1
ΩNight Heat #9
ΩBeyond Temptation #25
ΩRisky Pleasures #37
ΩIrresistible Forces #89
ΩIntimate Seduction #145
ΩHidden Pleasures #189
ΩA Steele for Christmas #253
ΩPrivate Arrangements #269

 *The Westmorelands
ΔMadaris Family Saga
ΩSteele Family titles

Other titles by this author
are available in ebook format.

BRENDA JACKSON

is a die "heart" romantic who married her childhood sweetheart and still proudly wears the "going steady" ring he gave her when she was fifteen. Because she believes in the power of love, Brenda's stories always have happy endings. In her real-life love story, Brenda and her husband of more than forty years live in Jacksonville, Florida, and have two sons.

A *New York Times* bestselling author of more than seventy-five romance titles, Brenda is a recent retiree who now divides her time between family, writing and traveling with Gerald. You may write Brenda at P.O. Box 28267, Jacksonville, Florida 32226, by email at WriterBJackson@aol.com or visit her website at www.brendajackson.net.

THE DENVER WESTMORELAND FAMILY TREE

Raphel and Gemma Westmoreland

Stern Westmoreland (Paula Bailey)

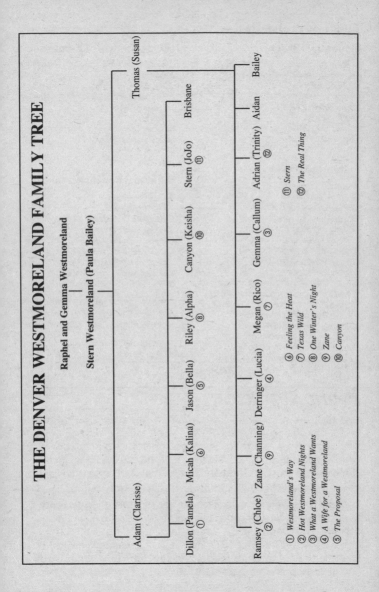

① Westmoreland's Way
② Hot Westmoreland Nights
③ What a Westmoreland Wants
④ A Wife for a Westmoreland
⑤ The Proposal
⑥ Feeling the Heat
⑦ Texas Wild
⑧ One Winter's Night
⑨ Zane
⑩ Canyon
⑪ Stern
⑫ The Real Thing

One

"I understand you're in a jam and might need my help."

In a jam was putting it mildly, Trinity Matthews thought, looking across the table at Adrian Westmoreland.

If only what he'd said wasn't true. And…if only Adrian wasn't so good-looking. Then thinking about what she needed him to do wouldn't be so hard.

When she and Adrian had first met, last year at his cousin Riley's wedding, he had been standing in a group of Westmoreland men. She had sized up his brothers and cousins, but had definitely noticed Adrian standing beside his identical twin brother, Aidan.

Trinity had found out years ago, when her sister Tara had married Thorn Westmoreland, that all Westmoreland men were eye candy of the most delectable kind. Therefore, she hadn't really been surprised to discover that Thorn's cousins from Denver had a lot of the same traits—handsome facial features, tall height, a hard-muscled body and an aura of primal masculinity.

But she'd never thought she'd be in a position to date one of those men—even if it was only a temporary ruse.

Trinity knew Tara had already given Adrian some details about the situation and now it was up to her to fill him in on the rest.

"Yes, I'm in a jam," Trinity said, releasing a frustrated breath. "I want to tell you about it, but first I want to thank you for agreeing to meet with me tonight."

He had suggested Laredo's Steak House. She had eaten here a few times, and the food was always excellent.

"No problem."

She paused, trying to ignore how the deep, husky sound of his voice stirred her already nervous stomach. "My goal," she began, "is to complete my residency at Denver Memorial and return to Bunnell, Florida, and work beside my father and brothers in their medical practice. That goal is being threatened by another physician, Dr. Casey Belvedere. He's a respected surgeon here in Denver. He—"

"Wants you."

Trinity's heart skipped a beat. Another Westmoreland trait she'd discovered: they didn't believe in mincing words.

"Yes. He wants an affair. I've done nothing to encourage his advances or to give him the impression I'm interested. I even lied and told him I was already involved with someone, but he won't let up. Now it's more than annoying. He's hinted that if I don't go along with it, he'll make my life at the hospital difficult."

She pushed her plate aside and took a sip of her wine. "I brought his unwanted advances to the attention of the top hospital administrator, and he's more or less dismissed my claim. Dr. Belvedere's family is well known in the city. Big philanthropists, I understand. Presently, the Belvederes are building a children's wing at the hospital that will bear their name. It's my guess that the hospital administrator feels that now is not the time to make waves with any of the Belvederes. He said I need to pick my battles carefully, and this is one I might not want to take on."

She paused. "So I came up with a plan." She chuckled

softly. "Let me rephrase that. Tara came up with the plan after I told her what was going on. It seems that she faced a similar situation when she was doing her residency in Kentucky. The only difference was that the hospital administrator supported her and made sure the doctor was released of his duties. I don't have that kind of support here because of the Belvedere name."

Adrian didn't say anything for a few moments. He broke eye contact with her and stared down into his glass of wine. Trinity couldn't help but wonder what he was thinking.

He looked back at her. "There is another solution to your problem, you know."

She lifted a brow. "There is?"

"You did say he's a surgeon, right?"

"Yes."

"Then I could break his hands so he'll never be able to use them in an operating room again."

She stared wide-eyed at him for a couple of seconds before leaning forward. "You're joking, right?"

"No. I am not joking. I'm dead serious."

She leaned back as she studied his features. They were etched with ruthlessness and his dark eyes were filled with callousness. It was only then that Trinity remembered Tara's tales about the twins, their baby sister, Bailey, and their younger cousin Bane. According to Tara, those four were the holy terrors of Denver while growing up and got into all kinds of trouble—malicious and otherwise.

But that was years ago. Now Bane was a navy SEAL, the twins were both Harvard graduates—Adrian obtained his PhD in engineering and Aidan completed medical school— and Bailey, the youngest of the four, was presently working on her MBA. However, it was quite obvious to Trinity that behind Adrian Westmoreland's chiseled good looks, irresistible charm and PhD was a man who could return to his old ways if the need arose.

"I don't think we need to go that far," she said, swallowing. "Like Tara suggested, we can pretend to be lovers and hope that works."

"If that's how you prefer handling it."

"Yes. And you don't have a problem going along with it? Foregoing dating other women for a while?"

He pushed his plate aside and leaned back in his chair. "Nope. I don't have a problem going along with it. Putting my social life on hold until this matter is resolved will be no big deal."

Trinity released a relieved sigh. She had heard that since he'd returned to Denver to work as one of the CEOs at his family-owned business, Blue Ridge Land Management, Adrian had acquired a very active social life. There weren't many single Westmoreland men left in town. In fact, he was the only one. His cousin Stern was engaged to be married in a few months; Bane was away in the navy and Aidan was practicing medicine at a hospital in North Carolina. All the other Westmoreland men had married. Adrian would definitely be a catch for any woman. And they were coming after him from every direction, determined to hook a Westmoreland man; she'd heard he was having the time of his life letting them try.

Trinity was grateful she wasn't interested. The only reason she and Adrian were meeting was that she needed his help to pull off her plan. In fact, this was the first time they had seen each other since she'd moved to Denver eight months ago. She'd known when she accepted the internship at Denver Memorial last year that a slew of her sister's Westmoreland cousins-in-law lived here. She had met most of them at Riley's wedding. But most lived in a part of Denver referred to as Westmoreland Country and she lived in town. Though she had heard that when Adrian returned to Denver he had taken a place in town instead of moving to his family's homestead, more for privacy than anything else.

"I think we should put our plan into action now," he said, breaking into her thoughts.

He surprised her further when he took her hand in his and brought it to his lips while staring deeply into her eyes. She tried to ignore the intense fluttering in her stomach caused by his lips brushing against her skin.

"Why are you so anxious to begin?"

"It's simply a matter of timing," he said, bringing her hand to his lips yet again. "Don't look now but Dr. Casey Belvedere just walked in. He's seen us and is looking over here."

Let the show begin.

Adrian continued to stare deep into Trinity's eyes, sensing her nervousness. Although she had gone along with Tara's suggestion, he had a feeling she wasn't 100 percent on board with the idea of pretending to be his lover.

Although Dr. Belvedere was going about his pursuit all wrong, Adrian could understand the man wanting her. Hell, what man in his right mind wouldn't? Like her sister, Tara, Trinity was an incredibly beautiful woman. Ravishing didn't even come close to describing her.

When he'd first met Tara, years ago, the first thing out of his mouth was to ask if she had any sisters. Tara had smiled and replied, yes, she had a sister who was a senior in high school with plans to go to college to become a doctor.

Jeez. Had it been that long ago? He recalled the reaction of every single man at Riley's wedding when Trinity had showed up with Thorn and Tara. That's when he'd heard she would be moving to Denver for two years to work at the hospital.

"Are you sure it's him?" Trinity asked.

"Pretty positive," he said, studying her features. She

had creamy mahogany-colored skin, silky black hair that hung to her shoulders and the most gorgeous pair of light brown eyes he'd ever seen. "And it's just the way I planned it," he said.

She arched a brow. "The way you planned it?"

"Yes. After Tara called and told me about her idea, I decided to start right away. I found out from a reliable source that Belvedere frequents this place quite a bit, especially on Thursday nights."

"So that's why you suggested we have dinner here tonight?" she asked.

"Yes, that's the reason. The plan is for him to see us together, right?"

"Yes. I just wasn't prepared to run into him tonight. Hopefully all it will take is for him to see us together and—"

"Back off? Don't bank on that. The man wants you and, for some reason, he feels he has every right to have you. Getting him to leave you alone won't be easy. I still think I should just break his damn hands and be through with it."

"No."

He shrugged. "Your call. Now we should really do something to get his attention."

"What?"

"This." Adrian leaned in and kissed her.

Trinity was certain it was supposed to be a mere brush across the lips, but like magnets their mouths locked, fusing in passion so quickly that it consumed her senses.

To Trinity's way of thinking, the kiss had a potency that had her insides begging for more. Every part of her urged her to make sure this kiss didn't end anytime soon. But the clinking of dishes and silverware made her remember where they were and what they were doing. She slowly eased her mouth away from Adrian's.

She let out a slow breath. "I have a feeling that did more than get his attention. It might have pissed him off."

Adrian smiled. "Who cares? You're with me now and he won't do anything stupid. I dare him."

He motioned for the waiter to bring their check. "I think we've done enough playacting tonight," he said smoothly. "Ready to leave?"

"Yes."

Moments after taking care of their dinner bill, Adrian took Trinity's hand in his and led her out of the restaurant.

Two

"So how did things go with Trinity last night?"

Adrian glanced up to see his cousin Dillon. The business meeting Dillon had called that morning at Blue Ridge Land Management had ended and everyone had filed out, leaving him and Dillon alone.

He'd never thought of Dillon as a business tycoon until Adrian had returned home to work for the company his family owned. That's when he got to see his Denver cousin in action, wheeling and dealing to maintain Blue Ridge's ranking as a Fortune 500 company. Adrian had always just thought of him as Dillon, the man who'd kept the family together after a horrific tragedy.

Adrian's parents, as well as his uncle and aunt, had died in a plane crash more than twenty years ago, leaving Dillon, who was the oldest cousin, and Adrian's oldest brother, Ramsey, in charge of keeping the family of fifteen Westmorelands together. It hadn't been easy, and Adrian would be the first to confess that he, Aidan, Bane and Bailey, the youngest four, had deliberately made things hard. Coming home from school one day to be told they'd lost the four people who had meant the most to them had been worse than difficult. They hadn't handled their grief well. They had rebelled in ways Adrian was now ashamed of. But Dillon, Ramsey and the other family members hadn't given up on them, even when they truly should have. For that reason and many others, Adrian deeply loved his family. Especially Dillon, who had taken on the State of Colorado when it had tried to force the youngest four into foster homes.

"Things went well, I think," Adrian said, not wondering how Dillon knew about the dinner date with Trinity even when Adrian hadn't mentioned anything about it. Dillon spoke to their Atlanta cousins on a regular basis, especially Thorn Westmoreland. Adrian figured Tara had mentioned the plan to Thorn and he had passed the information on to Dillon.

"Glad to hear it," Dillon said, gathering up his papers. "Hopefully it will work. Even so, I personally have a problem with the hospital administrator not doing anything about Dr. Belvedere. I don't give a damn how much money his family has or that they have a wing bearing their name under construction at the hospital. Sexual harassment is sexual harassment, and it's something no one should have to tolerate. What's happening to Trinity shouldn't happen to anyone."

Adrian agreed. If he had anything to do with it, Trinity wouldn't have to tolerate it. "We'll give Tara's idea a shot and if it doesn't work, then—"

"Then the Westmorelands will handle it, Adrian, the right way…with the law on our side. I don't want you doing anything that will get you in trouble. Those days are over."

Adrian didn't say anything as he remembered *those* days. "I won't do anything to get into trouble." He figured it was best not to say those days were completely over, especially after the suggestion he'd made to Trinity about breaking Belvedere's hands…something he'd been dead serious about. "Do you know anyone in the Belvedere family?" he asked Dillon.

"Dr. Belvedere's older brother Roger and I are on the boards of directors of a couple of major businesses in town, but we aren't exactly friends. He's arrogant, a little on the snobbish side. I heard it runs in the family."

"Too bad," Adrian said, rising from his chair.

"The Belvedere family made their money in the food industry, namely dairy products. I understand Roger has political aspirations and will announce his run for governor next month."

"I wish him the best. It's his brother Casey that I have a problem with," Adrian said, heading toward the door. "I'll see you later."

An hour later Adrian had finished an important report his cousin Canyon needed. Both Canyon and another cousin, Stern, were company attorneys. So far, Adrian was the only one from his parents' side of the Westmoreland tree who worked for Blue Ridge, the company founded by his and Dillon's father more than forty years ago.

At present there were fifteen Denver Westmorelands of his generation. His parents, Thomas and Susan Westmoreland, had had eight kids: five boys—Ramsey, Zane, Derringer and the twins, Adrian and Aidan—and three girls—Megan, Gemma and Bailey.

His uncle Adam and aunt Clarisse had had seven sons: Dillon, Micah, Jason, Riley, Canyon, Stern and Bane. The family was a close-knit one and usually got together on Friday nights at Dillon's place for a chow-down, where they ate good food and caught up on family matters. Dates had kept Adrian from attending the last two, but now, since he was *supposedly* involved with Trinity, his dating days were over for a while.

He tossed an ink pen on his desk before leaning back in his chair. For the umpteenth time that day he was reminded of the kiss he'd shared with Trinity last night. A kiss he had taken before she'd been aware he was about to do so. Adrian didn't have to wonder what had driven him. He could try to convince himself he'd only done it to rile Belvedere, but Adrian knew it was about more than that.

It all started when he had arrived at Trinity's place to pick her up. She must have been watching for him out the window of the house she was leasing because after he'd pulled into her driveway, before he could get out of his car, she had opened the door and strolled down the walk toward him.

He'd had to fight to keep his predatory smile from showing a full set of teeth. Damn, she had looked good. He could say it was the pretty, paisley print maxi dress that swirled around her ankles as she'd walked, or the blue stilettos and matching purse. He could say it was the way she'd worn her hair down to her shoulders, emphasizing gorgeous facial bones. Whatever it was, she had looked even more appealing than when he'd seen her at Riley and Alpha's wedding.

Adrian sucked in a sharp breath as more memories swept through his mind. Never had a woman's mouth tasted so delectable, so irresistibly sweet. She had been pretty quiet on the drive back to her place last night. Just as well, since his body had been on fire for her. Big mistake. How was he supposed to stop Belvedere from getting his hands on her when all he could think about was getting his own hands on her?

He stood and stretched his tall frame. After shoving his hands into the pockets of his pants, he walked over to the window and looked out at downtown Denver. When Tara had called him with the idea of pretending to be Trinity's lover, he had shrugged, thinking no problem, no big deal. A piece of cake. What he hadn't counted on was his own attraction to Trinity. It was taking over his thoughts. And that wasn't good.

Frustrated, he rubbed his hand down his face. He had to have more control. She wasn't the first woman he'd been attracted to and she wouldn't be the last. Taking another deep breath, he glanced at his watch. He was having dinner at McKays with Bailey and figured he would surprise her this time by being on time.

He had one more file to read, which wouldn't take long. Then, before leaving for the day, he would call Trinity to see how things had gone at work. He wanted to make sure Belvedere hadn't caused her any grief about seeing them together last night at Laredo's.

"So how did things go last night with Adrian?"

Trinity plopped down on the sofa in her living room after a long day at work. She'd figured she would hear from Tara sooner or later, who would want details.

"Great! We got to know each other while eating a delicious steak dinner. And Dr. Belvedere was off today, which was a good thing, given that he saw me and Adrian together last night at dinner."

"He did?"

"Yes."

"Coincidence or planned?"

"Planned. It seemed Adrian didn't waste time. Once he had agreed with your suggestion he found out where Belvedere liked to hang out and suggested we go there. Only thing, Adrian didn't tell me about his plan beforehand and when Dr. Belvedere walked in, I was unprepared."

"I can imagine. But you do want to bring this situation to a conclusion as quickly as possible, right?"

"Yes. But…"

"But what?"

"I hadn't counted on a few things."

"A few things like what, Trinity?"

Trinity nibbled on her bottom lip, trying to decide how much information she should share with her sister. Although there was a ten-year difference in their ages, they had always been close. Even when Tara had left home for college and medical school, Trinity had known her sister would return home often. After all, Derrick Hayes—the man Tara had dated since high school and had been engaged to marry—lived there.

But then came the awful day of Tara's wedding. Her sister had looked beautiful. She'd walked down the aisle on their father's arm looking as radiant as any bride could look. Trinity had been in her early teens and seeing Tara in such a beautiful gown had made her dream of her own wedding day.

But then, before the preacher could get things started, Derrick had stopped the wedding. In front of everyone, he'd stated that he couldn't go through with the ceremony because he didn't love Tara. He loved Danielle, Tara's best friend and maid of honor.

Trinity would never forget the hurt, pain and humiliation she'd seen in her sister's eyes and the tears that had flowed down Tara's cheeks when Derrick took Danielle's hand and the two of them raced happily out of the church, leaving Tara standing behind.

That night Tara had left Bunnell, and it had been two years before she had returned. And when she had, motorcycle celebrity Thorn Westmoreland had given her a public proposal the town was still talking about ten years later. Trinity's brother-in-law had somewhat restored her faith in men. He was the best, and she knew that he loved her sister deeply.

"Trinity? A few things like what?" Tara repeated, pulling Trinity's concentration back to the present.

"Nothing, other than I wish Adrian wasn't so darn attractive. You wouldn't believe the number of women staring at him last night."

She decided not to mention the fact that he had kissed her right in front of a few of those women, although he'd done it for Dr. Belvedere's benefit. She hadn't expected the kiss and she had gone to bed last night thinking about it. Today things hadn't been much better. Burying herself in work hadn't helped her forget.

"Yes, he is definitely handsome. Most Westmoreland men are. And don't worry about other women. He's single, but now that he has agreed to pretend to be your boyfriend, he's going to give you all his attention."

Trinity sighed. In a way, that's what she was afraid of. "Adrian doesn't think Dr. Belvedere seeing us together once will do it."

"Probably not, especially if the man is obsessed with having you. From what you've told me, it sounds like he is."

Trinity didn't say anything for a minute. "Well, I hope he gets the message because Adrian is serious about making sure the plan works."

"Good. I think you're in good hands."

Trinity wasn't so sure that was a positive thing, especially when she remembered the number of times last night she had thought about Adrian's hands. He had beautiful fingers, long and lean. She had wondered more than once how those fingers would feel stroking her skin.

"Trinity?"

She blinked, realizing she had been daydreaming. "Yes?"

"You're still keeping that journal, right?"

Tara had suggested she keep a record of each and every time Casey Belvedere made unwanted advances toward her. "Yes, I'm still keeping the journal."

"Good. Don't worry about anything. I wouldn't have suggested Adrian if I didn't believe he would be the right one to help handle your business."

"I know. I know. But..."

"But what?"

Trinity breathed in deeply. "But nothing. I just hope your idea eventually works."

"Me, too. And if it doesn't we move to plan B."

Trinity lifted a brow. "What's plan B?"

"I haven't thought of it yet."

She couldn't help but laugh. She loved her big sister and appreciated Tara being there for her right now. "Hopefully, there won't have to be a plan B."

"Let's keep hoping. In the meantime, just enjoy Adrian. He's a fun guy and you haven't had any fun lately. I know how it is, going through residency. Been there. Done that. You can only take so much and do so much. We're doctors, not miracle workers, Trinity. We have lives, too, and everybody needs downtime. Stress can kill—remember that."

"I will."

A few moments later she had ended her call with Tara and was about to head for the kitchen to put together a salad for dinner when her cell phone rang again. Trinity's heartbeat quickened when she saw it was Adrian.

What was that shiver about, the one that had just passed through her whole body? She frowned, wondering what was wrong with her. Why was she reacting this way to his phone call? It wasn't as if their affair was the real thing. Why did she feel the need to remind herself that it was only a sham for Dr. Belvedere's benefit?

She clicked on her phone. "Hello?"

"Hello, this is Adrian. How did things go at work today?"

She wished he didn't sound as good as he looked. Or that when he had arrived to pick her up for dinner last night, he'd not dressed as though he'd jumped right off the page of a men's magazine.

She had been ready to walk out the moment his car had pulled into her driveway. So there had been no reason for him to get out of his car to meet her halfway down the walkway. But he had done so, showing impeccable manners by escorting her to his car and opening the door for her. However, it wasn't his manners the woman in her had appreciated the most. He was so tall she had to look up at him, into a pair of eyes and a face that had almost taken her breath away.

She sighed softly now as the memory rushed through her mind. Only then did she recall the question he had asked her.

"Today was okay, probably because Dr. Belvedere is off for the next two days so I didn't see him. I'm dreading Friday when he returns."

"Hopefully things won't be so bad. We'll keep up our charade until he accepts the fact that you already have a man."

A pretend man but, oh, what a man, she thought to herself. "Do you think after seeing us together last night he believes we're an item?"

"Oh, I'm sure he probably believes it. But for him to accept it is a whole other story. It's my guess that he won't."

Trinity nibbled on her bottom lip. "I hope you're wrong."

"I hope I'm wrong, as well. Enjoy tomorrow and we'll see what happens on Friday. Just to be on the safe side, let's plan a date for the weekend. How about a show Saturday night?"

"A show?"

"Yes, one of those live shows at the Dunning Theater. A real casual affair."

She thought about what Tara had said, about Trinity getting out more and not working so hard. Besides, she and Adrian needed to be seen around town together as much as possible for Dr. Belvedere to get the message. "Do you think Belvedere will be attending the show, as well?"

He chuckled, and Trinity's skin reacted to the sound. Goose bumps formed on her arm. "Not sure, but it doesn't matter. The more we're seen together by others, the more believable our story will be. So are you good for Saturday night?"

"Yes. It just so happens I'm off this weekend."

"Good. I'll pick you up around seven."

Three

This is just a pretend date, so why am I getting all worked up over it? Trinity asked herself as she threw yet another outfit from her closet across her bed.

So far, just like all the other outfits she'd given the boot, it was either too dressy, not dressy enough or just plain boring. Frustrated, she ran her hands through her hair, wishing she had her sister's gift for fashion. Whenever Tara and Thorn went out on the town they were decked out to the nines and always looked good together. But even before Tara had become Mrs. Thorn Westmoreland, people had said she looked more like a model than a pediatrician.

Trinity glanced at her watch. Only an hour before Adrian arrived and she had yet to find an outfit she liked. Who was she kidding? A part of her was hoping that whatever she liked he would like, as well. She seldom dated and now, thanks to Casey Belvedere, it was being forced upon her.

Maybe she should call Adrian and cancel. Immediately she dismissed the idea from her mind. So far the week had been going smoothly. Dr. Belvedere had been off, even on Friday. It seemed everyone had breathed a lot easier, able to be attentive but relaxed. No one had had to look over their shoulders, dreading the moment when Belvedere showed his face. She wasn't the only one who thought he was a pain in the rear end.

Deciding she would take Tara's advice and have fun for a change, Trinity settled on a pair of jeans and a green pullover sweater. Giving both a nod of approval, she placed them across the chair. It was the middle of March and back home in Florida people were strutting around in tank tops and blouses. But in Denver everyone was still wearing winter clothes.

Trinity doubted she would ever get used to this weather.

"Which is why getting through your residency is a must," she mumbled to herself as she headed for the bathroom to take a shower. "Then you can leave and head back to Florida where you belong."

A short while later she had finished her shower, dressed and placed light makeup on her face. She smiled as she looked at herself in the mirror, satisfied with what she saw. No telling how many dates Adrian was giving up by pretending to be her man. The least she could do was make sure she looked worth his time and effort in helping her out.

She glanced at her watch. She had twenty minutes, and the last thing she had to do was her hair. She was about to pull the curling iron from a drawer when her cell phone rang, and she saw it was Adrian. She wondered if he was calling to say something had come up and he couldn't take her out after all.

"Hello?"

"Trinity?"

She ignored the sensations floating around her stomach and the thought of how good he sounded whenever he pronounced her name. "Yes?"

"I'm here."

She lifted a brow. "Where?"

"At your front door."

"Oh." She swallowed. "You're early."

"Is that a problem?"

She glanced at herself in the mirror. "I haven't done my hair yet."

"I have three sisters, so I understand. I can wait...inside."

Trinity swallowed again. Of course he would expect to wait inside. To have him wait outside in the car for her would be downright tacky. "Okay, I'm on my way to the door."

Glad she was at least fully dressed, she left her bedroom and moved toward the door despising the tingle that continued to sweep through her body. "Get a grip, girl. It's just Adrian. He's almost family," she told herself.

But when she opened the door the thought that quickly went through her mind was, *Scratch the thought he's almost family.*

As her gaze swept across him from top to bottom, she willed herself not to react to what she saw and failed miserably. She was mesmerized. If she thought he'd looked good in his business suit days ago, tonight his manliness was showing to the nth degree. There was just something about a tall, handsome man in a pair of jeans, white shirt and dark brown corduroy blazer. The Stetson on his head only added to the eye-candy effect.

"Now I see what you mean, so please do something with your hair."

His comment had her reaching for the thick strands that flowed past her shoulders. When she saw the teasing smile on his lips, she couldn't help but smile back as she stepped aside to let him in. "That bad?"

"No. There's nothing wrong with your hair. It looks great."

She rolled her eyes as she led him to her living room. "There're no curls in it."

He chuckled. "Curls aren't everything. Trust me, I know. Like I said, I have three sisters."

And she knew his sisters and liked them immensely. "Would you like something to drink while you wait?"

"Um, what do you have?"

"Soda, beer, wine and lemonade."

"I'll take a soda."

"One soda coming up," she said, walking off, and although she was tempted to do so, she didn't look back.

When she opened the refrigerator, the blast of cold air cooled her somewhat; she couldn't believe she'd actually gotten hot just looking at him. Closing the refrigerator, she paused. Some sort of raw, erotic power had emanated off him and she inwardly admitted that Adrian Westmoreland was an astonishing specimen of masculinity. The kind that made her want to lick him all over.

"Nice place."

She jerked around to find the object of her intense desire standing in the middle of her kitchen. For some reason he appeared taller, bigger than life and even sexier. "As you can see there's not much to it. It was either get a bigger place and share it with someone or get this one, which I can afford on my own."

He nodded. "It suits you."

She handed him the drink and their hands touched slightly. She hoped he hadn't noticed the tremble that passed through her with the exchange. "In what way?"

His gaze gave her body a timeless sweep and she felt her heartbeat quicken. His eyes returned to hers as he took his glass. "Nice. Tidy. Perfect coloring with everything blending together rather nicely."

Was she imagining things or had Adrian's eyes darkened to a deep, rich chocolate? And was his comparison of her to her home meant to be flirtatious? "Enjoy your soda while I work on my hair."

"Need help?"

She smiled as she quickly headed out of the kitchen. She

didn't want to imagine how his hands would feel on her head. "No, thanks. I can manage."

Adrian took a long sip of his drink as he watched Trinity leave her kitchen. Nice-looking backside, he thought, and then wished he hadn't. Tara would skin him alive if he made a play for her sister. And if Tara told Thorn, there would be no hope for Adrian since everybody knew Thorn was a man not to toy with.

Then why did you flirt with Trinity just now? he asked himself, taking another sip. *You're only asking for trouble. Your job is to pretend the two of you are lovers and not lust after her like some horny ass. You've already crossed the line with that kiss—don't make matters worse.*

He took another sip of his soda. What could be worse than wanting a woman and not being able to have her? A smile touched his lips, thinking that Dr. Casey Belvedere would soon find out.

"I'm ready."

He turned slightly and almost choked on the liquid he'd just sipped. She'd used one of those styling-irons to put curls in her hair at the ends. The style looked good on her. She looked good. All over. Top to bottom.

"You look nice."

"Thanks. You look nice yourself. You didn't say what show we'll be seeing."

"I didn't? Then I guess it will be a surprise. I talked to Tara earlier today and asked her about your favorite dessert. She told me about your fascination with strawberry cheesecake, so I made arrangements for us to stop for cheesecake and coffee on our way back."

"That's thoughtful of you."

"I'm a thoughtful person. You ready to go?"

"Yes."

He placed the empty glass on the counter and crossed the room to link his arm with hers. "Then let's go."

"You're driving a different car tonight," Trinity noted when they reached the sleek and sassy vehicle parked in her driveway. The night he'd taken her to dinner he'd been driving a black Lexus sedan. Tonight he was in a sporty candy-apple-red Lexus two-seater convertible.

"And I own neither. A good friend owns a Lexus dealership in town and when I returned to Denver he sold me a Lexus SUV. But he figures as much as I'm seen around town with the ladies that he might as well let me use any car off his lot whenever I go out on a date. He's convinced showcasing his cars around town is good publicity. And it has paid off. Several people have come into his dealership to buy his cars."

"And I bet most were women."

He chuckled as he opened the door for her. "Now why would you think that?"

"A hunch. Am I right?"

"Possibly."

"Go ahead and admit it. It's okay. I've heard all about your dating history," she said, buckling her seat belt.

"Have you?" he asked, leaning against the open car door.

"Yes."

"From who?"

"I'd rather not disclose my sources."

"And you think they're reliable?" he asked.

"I see no reason why they shouldn't be."

He shrugged before closing the door. She watched him sprint around the front to the driver's side to get in. He buckled his own seat belt, but before pressing the key switch he glanced over at her. "There's only one reliable source when it comes to me, Trinity."

She lifted a brow. "And who might that be?"

He pointed a finger at his chest. "Me. Feel free to ask me anything you want…within reason."

She smiled. "Then here's my first question. More women have purchased cars from your friend than men, right?"

He returned her smile as he backed out of her driveway. "I'll admit that they have."

"I'm not surprised."

"Why not?"

"Several reasons," she said, noticing the smooth sound of the car's engine as he drove down her street.

"State them."

She glanced over at him. He had brought the car to a stop at a traffic light. "I can see where some women would find you persuasive and lap up anything you say as gospel."

A smile she wouldn't categorize as *totally* conceited touched his lips. "You think so? You believe I might have that much influence?"

"Yes, but mind you, I said *some* women."

"What about you? Are you ready for a new car?"

She held his gaze. "Unless it's free, I'm not interested. A car payment is the last thing I need right now. The car I presently drive is just fine. It gets me from point A to point B and if I sing to it real nice, it might even make it to point C. I can't ask for anything more than that."

"You can but you won't."

His comment was right on the money but she wondered how he'd figured that out. "Why do you say that?"

The car was moving again and he didn't answer until when they reached another traffic light a few moments later. He looked over at her. "You're not the only one with sources. I understand that beneath those curls on your head is a very independent mind."

She shrugged as she broke away from his look to glance out the window. "I can't handle my business any other way. My parents raised all of us to be independent thinkers."

"Is that why you didn't go along with Tara's plan at first?"

She looked back at him. "You'll have to admit it's a little far-fetched."

"I look at it as a means to an end."

"I just hope it works."

"It will."

She was about to ask why he felt so certain when she noticed they had pulled up for valet parking. The building was beautiful and the architecture probably dated back to the eighteen hundreds. Freestanding, it stood as an immaculate building with a backdrop of mountains. "Nice."

"Glad you like it. It was an old hotel. Now it's been renovated, turned into a theater that has live shows. Pam's group is working on a production that will be performed here."

Trinity knew Dillon's wife, Pam, used to be a movie star who now owned an acting school in town. "That's wonderful."

"I think so, too. Her group is working hard with rehearsals and all. It will be their first show."

When they reached the ticket booth the clerk greeted Adrian by name. "Good evening, Mr. Westmoreland."

"Hello, Paul. I believe you're holding reserved tickets for me."

"Yes sir," the man said, handing Adrian an envelope. Adrian checked the contents before smiling at her. "We're a little early so we might as well grab a drink. They serve refreshments while we wait."

"Okay."

When they entered the huge room, Trinity glanced around. This area of the building was nicely decorated, as well.

"What would you like?" Adrian asked her.

"What are you drinking?"

"Beer."

"Then I'll take one, as well."

Adrian grabbed the attention of one of the waiters and gave him their order. It was then that a couple passed and Adrian said, "Roger? Is that you?"

A man who looked to be in his late thirties or early forties turned and gave Adrian a curious glance. "Yes, I'm Roger. But forgive me, I can't remember where we've met."

Adrian held out his hand. "Adrian Westmoreland. We've met through my brother Dillon," he lied, knowing the man probably wouldn't remember but would pretend that he did.

A huge smiled appeared on the man's face as he accepted Adrian's handshake. "Oh, yes, of course. I remember now. And this is my wife Kathy," he said, introducing the woman with him.

Adrian shook her hand. He then turned to Trinity and smiled. "And this is a very *special* friend," he said. "Roger and Kathy, I'd like you to meet Dr. Trinity Matthews."

Trinity couldn't help wondering what was going on in that mind of Adrian's. She soon found out when he said, "Trinity, I'd like you to meet Roger and Kathy Belvedere."

Trinity forced herself not to blink in surprise as she shook the couple's hands. "Nice to meet you."

"Likewise," Roger said, smiling. "And where do you practice, doctor? I'm familiar with a number of hospitals in the city. In fact," he said, chuckling and then bragging, "my family is building a wing at Denver Memorial."

"That's where I work. I'm in pediatrics, so I'm familiar with the wing under construction. It's much needed and will be nice when it's finished," Trinity said.

Roger's smile widened. "Thanks. If you work at Denver Memorial then you must know my brother Casey. He's a surgeon there. I'm sure you've heard of Dr. Casey Belvedere."

Trinity fought to keep a straight face. "Yes, I know Dr. Belvedere."

"Then I must mention to him that Kathy and I ran into the two of you."

"Yes, you do that," Adrian said, smiling.

After the couple walked off, the waiter approached with their beers. Trinity looked over at Adrian. "You knew he was going to be here tonight, didn't you?"

He looked at her. "Yes. And there's no doubt in my mind he'll mention seeing us to his brother."

Trinity nodded as she took a sip of her beer. Tonight was just another strategic move in Adrian's game plan. Why was she surprised…and sort of disappointed?

At that moment someone on a speaker announced that seating for the next show would start in fifteen minutes. As they finished their beers, she decided that regardless of the reason Adrian had brought her here, tonight she intended to enjoy herself.

Four

As he'd planned, after the show Adrian took Trinity to Andrew's, a place known in Denver for having the best desserts. While enjoying strawberry cheesecake topped with vanilla ice cream, Adrian decided he liked hearing the sound of Trinity's voice.

She kept the conversation interesting by telling him about her family. Her father owned a medical practice and her mother worked as his nurse. Her two older brothers were doctors, as well, living in Bunnell.

She also talked about her college days and how she'd wanted to stick close to home, which was why she'd attended the local community college in Bunnell for two years before moving to Gainesville to attend the University of Florida. Although it was a college town, the city of Gainesville provided a small-town atmosphere. She'd enjoyed living there so much that she'd remained there for medical school.

She also told him how she preferred a small town to a big one, how she found Denver much too large and how she looked forward to finishing up her residency and moving back to Bunnell.

He leaned back in his chair after cleaning his plate, admitting the cake and ice cream had been delicious. "Aw, come on," he joked to Trinity. "Why don't you just come clean and admit that the real reason you want to hightail it back is because you have a guy waiting there for you."

She made a face. The way she scrunched her nose and pouted her lips was utterly cute. "That is totally not true... especially after what Derrick did to Tara. The last thing I'd have is a boyfriend that I believed would wait for me."

He had heard all about the Tara fiasco from one of his cousins, although he couldn't remember which one. He couldn't believe any man in his right mind would run off and leave someone as gorgeous as Tara Matthews Westmoreland standing in the middle of some church. What a fool.

"What happened to Tara has made you resentful and distrustful of giving your heart to a hometown guy?"

She shrugged her shoulders and unconsciously licked whipped cream off her fork. In an instant his stomach tightened. Sexual hunger stirred to life in his groin. He picked up his glass of water and almost drained it in one gulp.

"Worse than that. It taught me not to truly give my heart to any man, hometown or otherwise."

He studied her, seeing the seriousness behind the beautiful pair of eyes staring back at him. "But things worked out fine for Tara in the end, didn't they? She met Thorn."

He saw the slow smile replace her frown. "Yes, she did, and I'm glad. He's made her happy."

Adrian nodded. "So there are happy endings sometimes."

She finished off the last of her cake before saying, "Yes, sometimes, but not often enough for me to take a chance."

"So you don't ever intend to fall in love?"

"Not if I can help it. I told you what I want."

He nodded again. "To return to Bunnell and work alongside your father and brothers in their medical business."

"Yes."

He took another sip of his water when she moistened the top of her lip with the tip of her tongue. "What about your happiness?" he asked her, shifting slightly in his chair.

She lifted a brow. "My happiness?"

"Yes. Don't you want to have someone to grow old with?"

She turned the tables when she asked, "Don't you?"

He thought about the question. "I intend to date and enjoy life for as long as I can. I'm aware at some point I'll need to settle down, marry and have children, but at the moment there're enough Westmorelands handling that without me. It seemed every time I came home for spring break, I would have a wedding to attend or a new niece, nephew or second cousin being born."

"Speaking of cousins…mainly yours," she said as if to clarify. "I've heard the story of how the Denver Westmorelands connected with the Atlanta-based Westmorelands, but what about these other cousins that might be out there?"

He knew she was referring to the ongoing investigation by Megan's husband, Rico, who was a private investigator. "It seems my great-grandfather Raphel Westmoreland was involved with four women before marrying my great-grandmother Gemma. Three of the women have now been accounted for. It seemed none were his wives, although there's still one more to investigate for clarification."

He paused and then said, "Rico and Megan found out that one of the women, by the name of Clarice, had a baby by Raphel that he didn't know about. She died in a train derailment but not before she gave the child to another woman—a woman who'd lost her child and husband. A woman with the last name of Outlaw."

He could tell by the light in Trinity's eyes that she found what he'd told her fascinating. He understood. He was convinced that if there were any more Westmoreland kin out there, Rico would find them.

Adrian glanced at his watch. "It's still early yet. Is there anything else you want to do before I take you home?"

She glanced at her own watch. "Early? It's almost midnight."

He smiled. "Is it past your bedtime?"

"No."

"Then plan to enjoy the night. And I've got just the place."

"Where?"

"Come on and I'll show you."

A half hour later Trinity was convinced she needed her head examined. She looked down at herself and wondered how she had let Adrian talk her into this. Indoor mountain climbing. Seriously?

But here she was, decked out with climbing shoes, a harness, a rope and all the other things she needed to scale a man-made wall that looked too much like the real thing.

"Ready?"

She glanced over at Adrian who was standing beside her, decked out in his own climbing gear.

Ready? He has to be kidding.

She saw the excitement in his eyes and figured this was something he liked doing on a routine basis. But personally, she was not an outdoorsy kind of girl.

So why did you allow him to talk you into it?

It might have had everything to do with the way he had grabbed hold of her hand as he'd led her out of Andrew's and toward his car. The tingling sensation that erupted the moment his hand touched hers had seemed to pulverize her common sense. Or it could have been the smile that would creep onto his lips whenever he was on an adrenaline high. Darn, it was contagious.

He snapped his fingers in front of her face, making her realize she hadn't answered his question. "Hey, don't start daydreaming on me now, Trinity. You need your full concentration for this."

She looked over at the fake mountain she was supposed to climb. He claimed this particular one was for beginners, but she had serious doubts about that. She glanced up at him. "I don't know about this, Adrian."

His smile widened and she felt the immediate pull in her stomach. "You can do this. You look physically fit enough."

She rolled her eyes. "Looks are deceiving."

"Then this will definitely get you in shape. But to be honest, I don't see where there needs to be improvement."

She swallowed. Had he just flirted with her for the second time that night? "So, have you ever climbed an outdoor mountain? The real thing?" she asked, rechecking the fit of her gloves.

"Sure. Plenty of times. I love doing it and you will, too."

She doubted it. Most people were probably in bed and here she was at one in the morning at some all-night indoor mountain climbing arena.

"Ready to try it?" Adrian asked, breaking into her thoughts.

"It's now or never, I suppose."

He smiled. "You'll do fine."

She wasn't sure about that, and did he *have* to be standing so close to her? "Okay, what do I do?"

"Just grab or step on each climbing hold located on the wooden boards as you work your way to the top."

She glanced up to the top and had to actually tilt her head back to see it. "This is my first time, Adrian. There's no way I'll make it that far up."

"You never know."

She did. She knew her limits…even when it concerned him. She was well aware that she was attracted to him just as she was well aware that it was an attraction that could get her into trouble if she didn't keep her sense about her.

Trinity moved toward the huge structure and proceeded to lift her leg. When she felt Adrian's hands on her backside, she jerked around and put her leg down. "What are you doing?"

"Giving you a boost. Don't you need one?"

She figured what she needed was her head examined. Had his intention been to give her a boost or to cop a feel? Unfortunately her backside didn't know the difference and it was still reacting to his touch. Heat had spiked in the area and was spreading all over.

"No, I don't need one, and watch your hands, Adrian. Keep them to yourself."

He gave her an innocent smile. "I am duly chastised. But honestly, I was only trying to help and was in no way trying to take advantage of a tempting opportunity."

"Whatever," she muttered, not believing him one bit. However, instead of belaboring the issue, she turned and started her climb, which wasn't easy.

Beginner's structure or no beginner's structure, it was meant to give a person a good workout. Why would anyone in their right mind want to do this for fun? she asked herself as she steadily and slowly moved up one climbing hold at a time. After each attempt she had to take a deep breath and silently pray for strength to continue. She had made it to the halfway point and was steadily moving higher.

"Looking good, Trinity. Real good."

It wasn't what he said but rather how he'd said it that made her turn slightly and look down at him, nearly losing her footing in the process. Climbing this structure was giving her backside a darn good workout. She could feel it in every movement, and there was no doubt in her mind that he could see it, too. While she was struggling to get to the top, he was down below ass-watching.

"That's it." Frustrated with him for looking and with

herself for actually liking the thought of him checking her out, she began her descent.

"Giving up already?"

She waited until her feet were on solid ground before she stood in front of him. Regarding him critically, she answered, "What do you think?"

Dark lashes were half lowered over his eyes when he said, "I think you're temptation, Trinity."

Whatever words she'd planned to say were zapped from her mind. Why did he have to say that and why had he said it while looking at her with those sexy eyes of his? The last thing she needed was for heat surges to flash through her body the way they were doing now.

"Considering the nature of our relationship, you're out of line, Adrian."

He leaned in closer and she got a whiff of his manly scent. She watched his lips curve into a seductive smile. "Why? And before you get all mouthy on me, there's something you need to consider."

"What?" she asked, getting even more frustrated. Although she would never admit it, she thought he was temptation, as well.

"I'm *supposed* to find you desirable. If I didn't, I couldn't pull off what needs to be done to dissuade Belvedere. My acting abilities can only extend so far. I can't pretend to want a woman if I don't."

Trinity went still. Was he saying he wanted her? From the way his gaze was darkening, she had a feeling that assumption was right. "I think we need to talk about it."

"At the moment, I think not."

When she opened her mouth to protest, he leaned in closer and said in a low, sexy tone, "See that structure over there?"

Her gaze followed his and she saw what he was referring to. It was huge, twice the size of the one she'd tried to scale, designed to challenge even the best of climbers. "Yes, I see it. What about it?"

The look on his face suddenly changed from desire to bold, heated lust. "I plan to climb all over it tonight. Otherwise, I'll try my damnedest later to climb all over you."

Five

Some words once stated couldn't be taken back. You just had to deal with them and Adrian was trying like hell to deal.

He had taken his climb and had done a damn good job scaling a wall he'd had difficulty doing in the past. It was amazing what lust could drive a man to do. And he was lusting after Trinity. Admitting it to her had made her nervous, wary of him, which was why she was hugging the passenger door as if it were her new best friend. If he didn't know for certain it was locked, he would be worried she would tumble out of the car.

"I won't bite," he finally said as he exited the expressway. *But I can perform a pretty good lick job,* he thought, but now was not the time to share such information.

"Pretending to be lovers isn't working, Adrian."

"What makes you think that?" he asked, although he was beginning to think along those same lines. "Because I admitted I want you, Trinity?"

"I would think that has a lot to do with it."

Adrian didn't say anything for a minute. Watching Trinity's backside while she'd climbed that wall had definitely done something to him; had brought out coiling arousal within his very core. And when the crotch of his jeans began pounding like hell from an erection he could barely control, he'd known he was in trouble. The only thing that had consumed his mind—although he knew better—was that he needed to have some of her.

"I thought I explained things to you, Trinity. You're a sexy woman. I'm a hot-blooded male. There're bound to be sparks."

"As long as those sparks don't cause a fire."

"They won't," he said easily. "I'll put it out before that happens. I'm no more interested in a real affair than you are. So relax. What I'm encountering is simple lust. I'll be thirty-one in a few months so I think I'm old enough to handle it." And he decided, starting now, he would handle it by taking control of himself, which is why he changed the subject.

"So what are your plans for tomorrow?" he asked.

He heard her sigh. "You mean *today,* right? Sunday. It's almost two in the morning," she said.

"I stand corrected. What are your plans for today?"

"Sleep, sleep and more sleep. I seldom get the weekends off and I can't wait to have a love affair with my bed. It will be Monday before you know it."

A love affair with her bed. Now why did she have to go there? Images of her naked under silken sheets were making his senses flare in the wrong directions.

He could imagine her scent. It would be close to what he was inhaling now but probably a little more sensual. And he could imagine how she would look naked. Lordy. His body throbbed at the vision. His fingers twitched. When he had touched her backside while giving her that boost he had actually felt the air thicken in his lungs.

"What about you? What do you have planned?"

If he was smart, he would go somewhere this weekend and get laid. Maybe that would help rid his mind of all these dangerous fantasies he was having. But he'd said on their first date that he would see her and only her until this ordeal with Belvedere was over. "Unlike you I won't be sleeping late. I promised Ramsey that I would help him put new fencing in the north range."

"I understand from Tara that you're not living on your family's land, that you lease a place in town."

"That's right. I'm not ready to build on my one hundred acres quite yet. Where I live is just what I need for now. I have someone coming in every week to keep things tidy and to prepare my meals, and that's good enough for me."

A short while later he was walking her to her door, although she'd told him doing so wasn't necessary. She had told him that the other night, as well, but he'd done so anyway.

He watched as she used her key to unlock the door. She then turned to him. "Thanks for a nice evening and for walking me to the door, Adrian."

"You're welcome. I'd like to check inside."

She rolled her eyes. "Is that really necessary?"

"I think so. After what happened with Keisha last year, I would feel a lot better if I did."

He figured she had heard how his cousin Canyon's wife, Keisha, had come home to find her house in shambles.

Trinity stepped aside. "Help yourself. I definitely want you to feel better."

Ignoring the sarcasm he heard in her voice, Adrian moved past her and checked the bedrooms, kitchen and bathrooms. He returned to the living room to find her leaning against the closed door, her arms crossed over her chest.

Her gaze clashed with his. "Satisfied?" she asked in an annoyed tone.

Suddenly a deep, fierce hunger stirred to life inside him. That same hunger he'd been hopelessly fighting all night. He told himself to walk out the door and not look back, but knew he could no more ignore the yearnings that were rushing through him than he could not breathe. She had no idea how totally sensuous she looked or the effect it was having on him.

He walked toward her in a measured pace. When she turned and reached for the door to open it for him to leave, he reached for her. The moment he touched her, fiery heat shot straight to his groin.

Before she could say anything, he pressed her back against the door and swooped his mouth down on hers with a hunger he needed to release. He couldn't recall precisely when she began kissing him back—all he knew was that she was doing so, and with a greed that equaled his.

He pressed hard into her middle, wanting her to feel just how aroused he was, as his tongue tangled with hers in a duel so sensuous he wasn't sure if the moans he heard were coming from her or from him.

No telling how long the kiss would have lasted if they hadn't needed to come up for air. He reluctantly released her mouth and stared down into the fierce darkness of her dazed eyes. She appeared stunned at the degree of passion the two of them had shared, which was even more than the last time they'd kissed.

He leaned in close to her moist lips and answered the question she'd asked him moments ago. "Yes, I'm satisfied, Trinity. I am now extremely satisfied."

He then opened the door and walked out.

Trinity stood there. Astonished.

What on earth had just happened? What was that sudden onslaught of intense need that had overtaken her, made her mold her mouth to his as though that was how it was supposed to be? And why did her mouth feel like it was where it belonged when it was connected to his?

She shook her head to jiggle out of her daze. The effects

were even more profound than before. It had taken days
to get her mind back on track after the last kiss; she had a
feeling this one would take even longer.

Her brows pulled together in annoyance. Why had he
kissed her again? Just as important, why had she let him?
She hadn't been an innocent bystander by any means. She
could recall every lick of his tongue just as she could remember every lick of hers.

She hadn't held back anything. She'd been just as ag-
gressive as he had. What did that say about her? What was
he assuming it said?

As she moved toward her bedroom to strip off her clothes
and take a shower, she couldn't help but recall something
else. Watching him climb that wall. He was in great shape
and it showed. He'd looked rough and so darn manly. Every
time he lifted a jeans-clad thigh as he moved upward, her
gaze had followed, watching how his muscles bulged and
showed the strength of his legs. The way his jeans had
cupped his backside had been a work of art, worthy to be
ogled. And when he removed his shirt, she had seen a perfect set of abs glistening with his sweat.

The woman in her had appreciated how he'd reached
the top with an overabundance of virility. That was probably why she'd lost her head the moment he'd taken her
into his arms and plowed her with a kiss that weakened
her knees. But now he was gone and once she got at least
eighteen hours of nonstop sleep, she would wake up in her
right mind.

She certainly hoped so.

Six

With little sleep and the memory of a kiss that just wouldn't let go, Adrian, along with his brothers and cousins, helped his older brother Ramsey repair fencing on a stretch of land that extended for miles.

Ramsey had worked as CEO for a while alongside Dillon before giving it up to pursue his first love: being a sheep rancher. Adrian's brothers Zane and Derringer preferred the outdoors, too. After working in the family business for a few years, Zane, Derringer and Ramsey, as well as their cousin Jason, joined their Montana Westmoreland cousins in a horse breeding and training business.

Ramsey's wife, Chloe, had arrived with sandwiches, iced tea and homemade cookies. Everyone teased Adrian's cousin Stern about his upcoming wedding to JoJo, who Stern had been best friends with for years. The two had been engaged for more than six months and Stern was anxious for the wedding to happen, saying he was tired of waiting.

Adrian didn't say anything as he listened to the easy camaraderie between his family. Leaving home for college had been hard, but luckily he and Aidan had decided to attend the same university. As usual, they had stuck together.

Their careers had eventually carried them in different directions. But Adrian knew that eventually his twin would return to Denver.

Aidan's plans were similar to Trinity's, regarding returning to her hometown to practice medicine. He could understand her wanting to do that, just as he understood Aidan. So why did the thought of her returning to Florida in about eighteen months bother him? It wasn't as if she meant anything to him. He'd already established the fact that she wasn't his type. They had nothing in common. She liked small towns and he preferred big cities. She wasn't an outdoor person and he was. So why was he allowing her to consume his thoughts the way she had been lately?

"So what's going on with you, Adrian? Or are you really Aidan?"

Adrian couldn't help but smile at his brother Zane. It seemed that while he had been daydreaming everyone had left lunch to return to work. "You know who I am and nothing's going on. I'm just trying to make it one day at a time."

"So things are working out for you at Blue Ridge?"

"Pretty much. I can see why you, Ramsey and Derringer decided the corporate life wasn't for you. You have to like it or otherwise you'd hate it."

Adrian liked his job as chief project officer. His duties included assisting Dillon when it came to any construction and engineering functions of the company, and advising him on the development of major projects and making sure all jobs were completed in a timely manner.

As they began walking to where the others were beginning work again, Zane asked, "So, how are things going being the pretend lover of Thorn's sister-in-law?"

Adrian glanced over at Zane, not surprised he knew. How many others in his family knew? Bailey hadn't mentioned anything the other night at dinner so she might be clueless. "Okay, I guess. I'm busy trying to establish this relationship with her for others to see. The first night I made sure the doctor saw us together and last night I went to a show that I knew one of his family members would be attending."

Zanc nodded. "Is it working?"

"Don't know yet. The doctor's path hasn't crossed with Trinity's since we started this farce."

"Hmm, I'm curious to see how things turn out."

Adrian looked at his brother. "If he's smart, he'll leave her alone."

"Oh, I'm not talking about her and thc doctor."

Adrian slowed his pace. "Then who are you talking about?"

Zane smiled. "The two of you."

Adrian stopped walking and Zane stopped, as well. "Don't know what you mean," he said.

Zane shrugged. "I saw her at Riley's wedding. She's a looker, but I expected no less with her being Tara's sister and all."

Adrian frowned. "So?"

Zane shoved his hands into the back pockets of his jeans. "So nothing. Forget I said anything. I guess we better get back to work if we want to finish up by dusk."

Adrian watched his brother walk off and decided that since he'd gotten married, Zane didn't talk much sense anymore.

"Dr. Matthews, I trust you've been doing well."

Immediately, Trinity's skin crawled at the sound of the man's voice as he approached her. She looked up from writing in a patient's chart. "Yes, Dr. Belvedere. I've been finc."

As a courtesy, she could ask him how he'd been, but she really didn't want to know. She tried ignoring him as she resumcd documenting the patient's chart.

"I saw you the other night."

Her heart rate increased. He had come to stand beside her. Way too close as far as she was concerned. She didn't look up at him but continued writing. "And what night was that?"

"That night you were out on a date at Laredo's."

She glanced up briefly. "Oh. I didn't see you." That was no lie since she had intentionally not looked in his direction.

"Well, I saw you. You were with a man," he said in an accusing tone.

She hugged the chart to her chest as she looked up again. "Yes, I was. If you recall, I told you I was involved with someone."

"I didn't believe you."

"I don't know why you wouldn't."

Belvedere smiled and Trinity knew the smile wasn't genuine. "Doesn't matter. Break things off with him."

Trinity blinked. "Excuse me?"

"You heard what I said."

Something within Trinity snapped. Not caring if anyone passing by heard her, she said, "I will not break things off with him! You have no right to dictate something like that to me."

A smirk appeared on his face before he looked over his shoulder to make sure no one was privy to their conversation. "I can make or break you, Dr. Matthews. If you rub me the wrong way, all those years you spent in medical school won't mean a damn thing. Think about it."

He turned to walk off, but then, as if he'd forgotten to say something, he turned back. "And the next time you decide to report me to someone, think twice. My family practically owns this hospital. I suggest you remember that. And to make sure we fully understand each other, I've requested your presence in the next two surgeries I have scheduled, which coincidently are on your next two days off. What a pity." Chuckling to himself, he walked off.

Trinity just stared at him. She felt as if steam were coming out of her ears. He'd just admitted to sabotaging her time off. *How dare he!*

Placing the patient's chart back on the rack, she angrily headed to the office of Wendell Fowler, the chief of pediatrics. Not bothering to wait on the elevator, she took the stairs. By the time she went up three flights of stairs she was even madder.

Dr. Fowler's secretary, an older woman by the name of Marissa Adams, glanced up when she saw her. "Yes, Dr. Matthews?"

"I'd like to see Dr. Fowler. It's important."

The woman nodded. "Please have a seat and I'll see if Dr. Fowler is available."

She hadn't been seated a few minutes when the secretary called out to her. "Dr. Fowler will see you now, Dr. Matthews."

"Thanks." Trinity walked around the woman's desk and headed for Wendell Fowler's office.

Less than a half hour later Trinity left Dr. Fowler's office unsatisfied. The man hadn't been any help. He'd even accused her of dramatizing the situation. He'd then tried to convince her that working in surgery on her days off under the guidance of Dr. Belvedere would be a boost to her medical career.

Feeling a degree of fury the likes of which she'd never felt before, she walked past Ms. Adams's desk with her head held high, fighting back tears in her eyes. If Dr. Belvedere's goal was to break her resolve and force her to give in to what he wanted, then he was wasting his time. If she had to give up her days off this week, she would do it. She refused to let anyone break her down.

Seven

Adrian leaned back in the chair behind his desk and stared at the phone he'd just hung up. He'd tried calling Trinity from a different number and she still wasn't taking his calls. He rubbed his hand across his jaw, feeling totally frustrated. So they had kissed. Twice. Big deal. That was no reason for her to get uptight about it and not take his calls. This was crap he didn't have time for.

It had been well over a week since that kiss. Ten days to be exact. He'd heard of women holding grudges but this was ridiculous. Over a kiss? Really? And no one could convince him she hadn't enjoyed it just as much as he had. All he had to do was close his eyes to relive the moments of all that tongue interaction. It had been everything a kiss should be and more.

The text signal on his cell phone indicated he had a message. He pulled the phone out of his desk drawer and tried to ignore the flutters that passed through his chest when he saw it was from Trinity.

Got your calls. Worked on my days off. Belvedere's orders. Spent last 10 days at hospital. Tired. Can barely stand. Off for few days starting tomorrow a.m.

Adrian sat straighter in his chair. What the hell! Trinity had worked on her days off? And it had been Belvedere's orders? Adrian's hands trembled in anger when he texted her back.

On my way 2 get you now!

She texted him back.

No. Don't. I'm okay. Just tired. Going home in the a.m. Will call you then.

Adrian frowned. If Trinity thought that message satisfied him, she was wrong. Who required anyone to work on their days off? There were labor laws against that sort of thing. And if Belvedere had ordered her to do so then the man had gone too damn far.

There was a knock on his office door.

"Come in."

Dillon stuck his head in. "I'm leaving early. Bailey's watching the kids while Pam and I enjoy a date night."

His cousin must have seen the deep scowl on Adrian's face. He stepped into the office and closed the door behind him, concern in his eyes. "What's wrong with you, Adrian?"

Adrian stood. Agitated, he paced in front of his desk. It was a few moments before he'd pulled himself together enough to answer Dillon's question. "I hadn't heard from Trinity in over a week and was concerned since I knew Belvedere had seen us together that night at dinner. She texted me a few moments ago. The man ordered her to work on her days off. She's worked ten days straight, Dil. Can you believe that?"

Before Dillon could answer, Adrian added, "I've got a

good mind to go to that hospital and beat the hell out of him."

"I think you need to have a seat and think this through."

The hard tone of Dillon's voice had Adrian staring at him. And then, as Dillon suggested, he sat. "I'm sitting, Dillon, but I still want to go over to that hospital and beat the hell out of Belvedere."

"Sure you do. But I'm telling you now the same thing I told you the day you came home after whipping Joel Gaffney's behind. You can't settle anything with a fight."

Maybe not, Adrian thought. But if he remembered correctly, he had felt a lot better seeing that bloody nose on Gaffney. Adrian had wanted to make sure Joel thought twice before putting a snake in Bailey's locker again. "It was either me or Bane," Adrian said. "And I'm sure Gaffney preferred my whipping to Bane's. Your kid brother would not have shown any mercy."

Dillon rolled his eyes. "Again, I repeat, you can't settle anything with a fight. Belvedere will file charges and you'll end up in jail. Then where will Trinity be?"

"Better off. I might be in jail, but when I finish with Belvedere he'll never perform surgery on anyone again. I'll see to it."

Dillon stared at him for a long moment before crossing the room to drop down in the chair across from Adrian's desk. "I think we need to talk."

"Not sure it will do any good. If I find out Belvedere made Trinity work on her off days just for spite, I'm going to make him wish he hadn't done that."

"Fine, then come up with a plan that's within the law, Adrian. But first know the facts and not assumptions. It could be that she was needed at the hospital. Doctors work all kinds of crazy hours. You have two siblings who are doctors so you should know that. Emergencies come up that have to be dealt with whether you're scheduled to be off or not."

Adrian knew what Dillon was trying to do. Come up with another plausible reason why Trinity had been ordered to work on her days off. "And what if I don't like the facts after hearing them?"

"Then like I said, come up with a plan. And if it's one that makes sense, you'll get my support. I don't appreciate any man trying to take advantage of a woman any more than you do. In the meantime, you stay out of trouble."

Dillon stood and headed for the door. Before he could open it, Adrian called out, "Thanks, Dil."

Dillon turned around. "Just do as I ask and stay out of trouble. Okay?"

"I'll try."

When Dillon gave him a pointed look Adrian knew that response hadn't been good enough. "Okay. Fine. I'll stay out of trouble."

Trinity believed that if she continued forcing one foot in front of the other she would eventually make it out of the hospital to the parking lot and into her car. But then she would have to force her eyes to stay open on the drive home.

Never had she felt so tired. Her body ached all over. Not from the hours it had missed sleep but because of the other assignments given to her on top of her regular job…all deliberately and for the sole purpose of making her give in to Dr. Belvedere's advances. If she'd ever had an inkling of attraction to him, did he really think she would let him touch her after this? Did it matter to him that she was beginning to hate him? He didn't see her as a colleague; all he saw was a body he wanted. A body he would do just about anything to get. A conquest.

When she stepped off the elevator on the main level, Belvedere stood there waiting to get on. Her eyes met his and she gritted her teeth when he had the nerve to smile. "Good morning, Dr. Matthews."

"Dr. Belvedere," she acknowledged and kept walking.

"Wait up a minute, Dr. Matthews."

She had a mind to keep walking, but it would have been a show of total disrespect for a revered surgeon, so she paused and turned. "Yes, Dr. Belvedere?"

He came to a stop in front of her. "Just wanted to say that you did a great job in surgery the other night."

"Thank you," she replied stiffly. She was tempted to tell him just what he could do with that compliment.

"I think we should have dinner to discuss a few things," he added smoothly. "I'll pick you up tonight at seven."

"Sorry, she has other plans."

Trinity's breath caught at the sound of the masculine voice. She turned to see Adrian walking toward them. Why was her heart suddenly fluttering like crazy at the sight of him? And why did seeing him give her a little more strength than she had just moments ago?

Even with the smile plastered on his lips, his smile didn't quite reach his eyes. He was angry. She could feel it. But he was holding that anger back and she appreciated that. The last thing she needed was him making a scene with one of her superiors.

Because of his long strides, he reached her in no time. "Adrian, I didn't expect to see you here."

He slid his arms around her waist, placed a kiss on her lips and hugged her. "Hey, baby. I figured the least I could do after you worked ten days straight is be here to take you home."

She glanced over at Dr. Belvedere and swallowed. Unlike Adrian, Dr. Belvedere wasn't smiling. She figured he realized that, dressed in blue scrubs, he failed miserably to compare to Adrian, who was wearing a designer suit that looked tailor-made for his body.

Before she could make introductions, Adrian turned to Belvedere. "Dr. Belvedere, right?" he asked, extending his hand to the man. "I've heard a lot about you. I'm Adrian Westmoreland, Trinity's significant other."

From the look that appeared in Belvedere's eyes, Adrian knew the man hadn't liked the role he'd claimed in Trinity's life. It took every ounce of control Adrian could muster to exchange handshakes with Belvedere. He wanted to do just what he'd told Dillon and beat the hell out of him. Even so, the memory of Dillon's advice kept him in line. Though he couldn't resist the opportunity to squeeze the man's hand harder than was needed. There was no way the doctor didn't know he'd purposely done so.

Let him know what I can do to those precious fingers of his if I'm riled.

Adrian turned back to Trinity and inwardly flinched when he saw tired eyes and lines of exhaustion etched into her features. He needed to get her out of here now before he was tempted to do something he would enjoy doing but might regret later. "Ready to go, baby?"

"Yes, but my car is here," she said, and he noticed that like him she had dismissed Dr. Belvedere's presence. Why the man was still standing there was beyond Adrian's comprehension.

"I'll come back for it later," he said, taking her hand. He didn't even bother to say anything to the doctor before walking away. He just couldn't get the words *It was nice meeting you* from his lips when they would have been a bald-faced lie.

When they exited the building Trinity paused and glanced up at him. "Thanks."

He knew what she was thanking him for. "It wasn't easy. Just knowing he had you work on your off days made me angry." He paused. "Were you needed or did he do it for spite?"

She looked away, and when she looked back at him, he saw the anger in her eyes. "He did it for spite."

If it wasn't for the talk he'd had with Dillon he would go back into the hospital and clean up the floor with Belvedere. But what Dillon had said was true. In the end, Adrian would be in jail and Belvedere would make matters worse for Trinity.

"Come on, my car is parked over there. I lucked out and got a spot close to the entrance."

"I'm glad. I don't recall the last time I was so tired. It wouldn't be so bad if I'd been able to sleep, but Belvedere made sure I stayed busy."

"The bastard," Adrian muttered under his breath.

"I heard that," she said. "And I concur. He is a bastard. What's so sad is that he actually thinks what he's doing is okay, and that in the end I'll happily fall into his arms. He's worse than a bastard, Adrian."

Adrian wasn't going to disagree with her. "We need to come up with a plan."

She chuckled softly and even then he could hear her exhaustion. "I thought we had a plan."

"Then we need a backup plan since he wants to be difficult."

"He actually told me to get rid of you, and told me he deliberately scheduled me on my days off. I went to see Dr. Fowler, who is chief of pediatrics, and he accused me of being dramatic. It's as though everyone refuses to do anything where Belvedere is concerned."

Adrian pulled her closer when they reached his car. He helped her inside and snapped her seat belt in place. "Go ahead, close your eyes and rest a bit. I'll wake you when I get you home."

* * *

Doing as Adrian suggested, Trinity closed her eyes. All she could do was visualize her bed—soft mattress, warm covers and a firm pillow. She needed to go to the grocery store to pick up a few things, but not today. Right now she preferred sleeping to eating. She would take a long, hot bath…not a shower…but a soak in her tub to ease the aches from her muscles. She planned to sleep for an entire day and put everything out of her mind.

Except.

Except the man who had showed up unexpectedly this morning to drive her home. Seeing him had caused her heart to thump hard in her chest and blood to rush crazily through her veins. She knew for certain she had never reacted to any other man that way before. That meant she was more exhausted than she had thought. And it was messing with her hormones.

Why this effect from Adrian and no one else? Why was Adrian's manly scent not only flowing through her nostrils but seeping into her pores and kicking sensations into a body that was too tired to respond?

In the deep recesses of her mind, she was trying not to remember the last time they'd been together. Namely, the kiss they'd shared. It had been the memory of that kiss that had lulled her to sleep when she'd thought she was too tired to close her eyes. The memory of that kiss was what she had thought about when she had needed to think of pleasant things to keep going.

There was no doubt in her mind that when it came to kissing, Adrian was definitely on top of his game. Even now, she remembered how his mouth had taken hers.

She had kissed him back, acquainting herself with the shape and fullness of his lips, his taste. It had been different from the first kiss. Longer. Sweeter. She had allowed herself to indulge. In doing so, it seemed her senses had gone through some sort of sensitivity training. Her head had been spinning and her tongue tingling. She'd been stunned by the force of passion that had run rampant through her.

Then there was the way he had held her in his arms. With his hands in the center of her back, he had held her with a possession that was astounding. She had felt every solid inch of him. Some parts harder than others, and it was those hard parts…one in particular…that had her fantasizing about him since.

"Wake up, Trinity. We're here."

She slowly opened her eyes. She glanced out the window at her surroundings. Slightly disoriented, she blinked and looked again before turning to Adrian. "This isn't my home."

A smile touched his lips. "No, it's mine. When I said I was taking you home, I meant to my place."

Now she was confused. She sat straighter in her seat. "Why?"

"So I can make sure you get your rest. Undisturbed. I wouldn't put it past Belvedere to find some excuse to call or show up at your place uninvited."

The thought of Dr. Belvedere doing either of those things bothered her. "Do you think he'd actually just drop by?"

"Not sure. But if he does, you won't be there. The man has issues and I wouldn't put anything past him."

Trinity hated saying it but neither would she. Still… To sleep at Adrian's place just didn't seem right. "I don't think it's a good idea for me to stay here."

"Why?"

She shrugged. "People might think things about us."

He chuckled. "People are *supposed* to think things about us, Trinity. The more they do, the better it is. Belvedere will look like a total ass trying to come on to a woman already seriously involved with another man. It will only show how pathetically demented he is."

What Adrian said made sense, but she was still wearing her scrubs and she wanted to get out of them. "I don't have any clothes."

"No problem. I'll loan you my T-shirt that will cover you past your thighs, and after you get a good day's rest, I'll take you to your place to get something else to put on. The main thing is for you to get some sleep. I'm going into the office once I get you settled in."

"I can't hide out here forever, Adrian."

"Not asking you to do that. I just think we need to continue to give the impression that we're lovers and not just two people merely seeing each other."

He paused a moment and then asked, "Why are you afraid to stay at my place?"

Good question.

"It's not that I'm afraid to stay here. It's just that I was looking forward to sleeping in my own bed."

An impish, feral smile curved his lips. "You might like mine better."

That's what I'm afraid of.

Why had his tone dropped a notch when he'd said that? His raspy words had resonated through her senses like a heated caress.

Quickly deciding all she wanted was to get some sleep, regardless of whose bed it was, she agreed. "Fine. Let's go. Your bed it is. And…Adrian?"

"Yes?"

"I sleep alone, so no funny business."

He chuckled. "I give you my word. I won't touch you unless you touch me first."

Then there shouldn't be any problems, she thought, because she wouldn't be touching him. At least she hoped not.

Eight

Adrian glanced around the conference room at the four other men sitting at the table. All wore intense expressions. Since joining the company and regularly attending executive board meetings, he'd discovered that they all wore that look when confronted with major decisions involving Blue Ridge Land Management.

Today's discussion was about a property they were interested in near Miami's South Beach. He'd given his report and now it was up to the board to decide the next move. It was Dillon who spoke, addressing his question to Adrian. "And you don't think a shopping complex there is a wise investment for us?"

"No, not from an engineering standpoint. Don't get me wrong, South Beach is a nice area, but there are several red flags such as labor issues and building costs that we don't want to deal with. One particular company is monopolizing the market and deliberately jacking up prices. It's not a situation we should get into right now. Besides, whatever development we place there will only be one of the same kind of complex that's already there. Even that's spelled out in the marketing report."

He knew his report hadn't been what they'd wanted to

hear. For years, Blue Ridge had tossed around the idea of building a huge shopping complex in South Beach. The timing hadn't been right then and, as he'd spelled out in his report, the timing wasn't right now.

Because he'd been taught that when he was faced with a problem he should be ready to offer a solution, he said, "There's a lucrative substitute in Florida that I'd like you to consider."

"And where might that be?" Riley asked, taking a sip of his coffee. "West Palm Beach?"

"No," Adrian replied. "Further north. It's one of the sea islands that stretches from South Carolina to Florida, right along the Florida coast. Amelia Island."

A smile touched Dillon's lips. "I went there once for a business conference. Took Pam with me and we stayed for a week. It's quaint, peaceful, totally relaxing…and—" his smile widened "—there are about six or seven beautiful golf courses."

"So I heard. And while you were enjoying your time on those golf courses, what was Pam doing?" Adrian inquired.

Dillon scrunched his forehead trying to remember. "She visited the spa a few times, otherwise she hung out by the pool reading."

"Just think of what choices she could have made if we had a complex on the island," Adrian said. "The clientele flocking to Amelia Island can afford to jet in on private planes, spend seven days golfing and dining at exclusive restaurants. They can certainly afford the type of luxury complex we want to build."

Adrian could tell he had their interest.

"What about labor issues and building costs?" Stern asked.

"Nearly nonexistent. The only problem we might run into is a few islanders not embracing change, who might want the island to remain as it is. But the person I spoke with this morning, who happens to be a college friend of mine who lives on the island, says that segment of the population is outnumbered by progressives who want the island to be a number-one vacation spot."

Providing everyone with the handouts he'd prepared, Adrian told them why placing a development on Amelia Island would work. A huge smile touched Canyon's face. "So, I suggest we see what we can do to make it happen."

An hour later, Adrian was back in his office. Since the meeting had been scheduled for ten o'clock, that had given him time to pick up Trinity from work and get her settled into his place. By the time he'd left for the office she was in his Jacuzzi tub. He expected that she was asleep now and that's what he wanted. That's what she needed.

And because his housekeeper had just been in, his place was in decent order and his refrigerator well stocked. Trinity had even complimented him on how neat and clean his place was and how spacious it was for just one person.

He had another meeting to attend today, a business dinner. But he was looking forward to returning home. Just to check on her, he told himself. Nothing more. She wasn't his first female houseguest and she wouldn't be the last. But then there was the fact that he had been thinking of her all day, when he hadn't wanted to. So what was that about?

He was pulling a folder from the In tray on his desk when his cell phone rang. He couldn't help smiling when he saw the caller was his twin.

"Yes, Dr. Westmoreland?"

The chuckle on the other end was rich. "Sounds good, doesn't it?"

"I always told you it would. How're things going?"

"Fine. When are you going to pay me a visit?"

Adrian leaned back in his chair. "I had planned to visit Charlotte this month but—"

"You're too involved with some female, right?"

Adrian chuckled. "Should I ask how you know?"

"You're letting off strong emotions."

Adrian didn't doubt it, and he blamed Belvedere for making him want to hurt somebody. "I have a lot going on here." He told his brother about the charade he and Trinity were playing.

"Trinity Matthews? I like her. I spent a lot of time talking to her at Riley's wedding."

"I noticed."

"Oops. Someone sounds jealous."

"No jealousy involved. Just saying I noticed the two of you had a lot to say to each other." He paused and added, "But I figured you were doing it to get a rise out of Jillian."

"If I was, it didn't work."

"Now what are you going to do?"

"Move on and not look back."

"Can you do that?" Adrian asked.

"I can try." Aidan paused. "Now back to you and Trinity. Has that doctor taken the bait and left her alone?"

"No, in fact he told her to break things off with me and when she refused he made her work longer hours and on her days off. And both days were assisting in surgery."

"Is the man crazy? An exhausted doctor can make costly mistakes, especially during surgery. The man isn't fit to be a doctor if getting a woman in his bed is more important than the welfare of his patients. That disgusts me."

"It disgusts me, as well," Adrian said. "That's why I refuse to let him use her that way."

"I'm feeling your emotions again. They are pretty damn strong, Adrian. Unless you plan on doing something with those feelings for Trinity then you should try keeping them in check."

"I suggest you do the same with Jillian," Adrian chided. "Just like you feel my emotions, remember I can also feel yours."

"I guess I do need to remember that."

After Adrian ended the call with his brother he couldn't help wondering if Aidan would be able to move on from his breakup with Jillian and not look back as he'd claimed. Adrian's thoughts shifted to Trinity. Was she still sleeping? The thought of her curled up in a bed in one of his guest rooms sent strong, heavy heartbeats thumping in his chest.

When he recalled how exhausted she was, barely able to stand on her feet, a muscle jumped in his jaw. No one should have to work in that state. All because Belvedere had tried breaking her down.

Anger poured through him at the thought. He was only soothed in knowing that for the time being she was safely tucked away under his roof. He rubbed the back of his neck. Aidan was right about keeping his emotions in check where Trinity was concerned. Doing so was hard, and he didn't like the implications of what that could mean. Especially when he was in a mad rush to leave the office and go home to see her. That wasn't good. He needed a diversion.

Adrian knew the one woman he could always count on. He picked up his phone and tapped in her number. He sighed in relief when she answered.

"Bailey Westmoreland."

"Bay? How would you like to do a movie tonight?"

He smiled when she said yes. "I have a business dinner in a few hours and will pick you up afterward. Around seven."

Trinity shifted in bed and curled into another position beneath the covers. When had her mattress begun to feel so soft? She slowly opened her eyes and looked around the room. Beautiful blue curtains hung at the window, the same shade as the bedspread covering her. Blue? Her curtains and bedcoverings weren't blue. They were brown. Pushing hair back from her face, she pulled herself up in a bed that wasn't hers. She then recalled where she was. Adrian's place.

Although she had been too exhausted to appreciate the décor when she'd first arrived, she remembered being impressed with the spaciousness of his condo as well as how tidy it was. He'd told her he had a housekeeper who came in twice a week, not only to keep the place looking decent, but also to do his laundry and prepare his meals.

That was a nice setup. Although she had a fetish for keeping her own place neat, she couldn't help but think about all the laundry she had yet to get to. And as far as cooked meals, she only got those when she went home to Bunnell. Otherwise she ate on the run, and mostly at fast-food places.

This was a nice guest room, she thought. Not too feminine and not too manly. The painting on the wall was abstract and she appreciated the splash of color that went with the drapes, the carpeting and the dark cherrywood furniture. There had been a lot of pillows on the bed, which she had tossed off before diving under the covers.

She pushed those same covers back as she eased out of bed, suddenly remembering that the only stitch of clothing she wore was the T-shirt Adrian had loaned her. It barely touched her mid-thigh. The material felt soft against her skin.

Moments later, after coming out of the connecting bathroom, she slid her shoulders into a silk bathrobe Adrian had placed across the arm of a chair. Her gaze lit on the clock on the nightstand. It was a little after seven. Had she really slept more than ten hours?

Since she felt well rested, she figured her body must have needed it. What had Belvedere been thinking to make her work such long hours, which was clearly against hospital policy? She knew very well what he'd been thinking and it only made her despise him that much more.

Her stomach growled and she left the bedroom for the kitchen. As she passed by several rooms on her way downstairs, she couldn't help but appreciate how beautiful they looked. When she got downstairs to the living room, she was surprised at the minimal furnishings. Although the place was more put-together than her own, it had the word "temporary" written all over it.

Once in the kitchen she opened the refrigerator and saw that Adrian's housekeeper had labeled the neatly arranged containers for each day of the week. Did that mean he ate in every day? What if he missed the meal for that day? Did it go to waste?

If that was true, today wouldn't be one of those days. She pulled out the container labeled for today and pulled off the top. *Mmm.* The pasta dish smelled good. Recalling that Adrian had told her to eat anything she wanted—and it seemed he definitely had more than enough to share— she spooned out a serving onto a plate to warm it in the microwave. Meals cooked and at your disposal was a working person's dream. Life couldn't get any better than this.

This kitchen was nice, with stainless steel appliances. She thought about her drab-looking kitchen and figured she could get used to living in this sort of place.

She ate her food, alone, and couldn't help but appreciate how Adrian had showed up at the hospital this morning to pick her up. He'd known her body would be racked with exhaustion and he had thought about her welfare. Dr. Belvedere, on the other hand, hadn't thought of anything but his own selfish motives.

Now that she was well rested, she recalled how Adrian had looked. Already dressed for work, he had been wearing a business suit that fitted perfectly over his broad shoulders, heavily muscled thighs and massive biceps. He had walked toward her with a swagger that had nearly taken her breath away. No man should have a right to look that good in the morning. His shirt had looked white and crisp, and the printed tie made a perfect complement. The phrase "dress to impress" had immediately come to mind, as well as *mind-blowingly sexy*.

It didn't take her long to eat the meal and tidy up the kitchen after loading the dishes in the dishwasher. The clock on the kitchen wall indicated it was almost eight. Adrian hadn't mentioned anything about working late. Now that she was rested she could go back to her place. Her only problem was that she didn't have her car.

She glanced down at herself. The bathrobe covered more than the T-shirt, but still, she didn't feel comfortable parading around any man's home not fully dressed. Going into the living room, she decided to call her sister with an update on what Belvedere had done.

"Why am I not surprised?" Tara said moments later. "He reminds me so much of that doctor in Kentucky who tried forcing me into a relationship with him. But Belvedere really did something unethical by forcing you to work. And the nerve of him telling you to end your relationship with Adrian. Just who does he think he is?"

"I don't know but his actions only make me despise him more. And he saw firsthand that I won't end things with Adrian this morning. Adrian came to the hospital to pick me up."

"Adrian picked you up from work?"

"Yes." Trinity proceeded to tell her sister how Adrian had been there to drive her and, instead of taking her home, had taken her to his place to get undisturbed sleep.

"That was nice of him."

"Yes, it was," Trinity said, glancing at the clock on the wall again. "He hasn't come home yet, so I guess he's working late." She wouldn't mention that she was slightly disappointed he hadn't called to check on her. "He'll be taking me home when he gets here."

"Well, I'm glad you got undisturbed sleep."

"I'm glad, too. I honestly needed it."

Trinity had washed the clothes she'd worn that morning and was tossing them in the dryer when she heard Adrian's key in the door lock. Finally he was home. It was close to ten o'clock and he'd known she was stranded at his place without her car. The least he could have done was call to see how she was doing, even if he needed to work late.

But what if he hadn't been working late? What if he'd been with someone on a date or something? She frowned, wondering why her mind was going there. And why she was feeling more than a tinge of jealousy.

Why are you trippin', Trinity? It's not as if you and Adrian got the real thing going on. It's just a charade. How many times do you have to remind yourself of that? On the other hand, he had said he wouldn't see anyone else.

"If the rules changed, he should have told me," she muttered angrily, leaving the laundry room and passing through his kitchen. She'd made it to the living room by the time he walked inside.

She willed herself not to show any reaction to how good he looked with his jacket slung across his shoulder. But then she noticed other things: his tie was off and she picked up the scent of a woman's perfume.

Trinity took a calming breath, thinking a degree of civility was required here. But then she lost it, and before Adrian had a chance to see her standing there, she said in an accusing tone, "You've been with someone."

Nine

The moment Adrian saw Trinity a jolt of sexual desire rocked him to the bone. She was angry, hands on hips, spine ramrod straight and wearing his bathrobe, which drooped at her shoulders and almost swallowed her whole. But damn, nothing would satisfy him more than to cross the room and kiss that angry look off her lips.

But, suddenly, it occurred to him that she had no right to be angry. She was the reason he hadn't come home when he could have. Too much temptation under his roof. Too many thoughts of her had floated through his head all day. He hadn't enjoyed the movie for thinking of her.

And what had she just accused him of? *Being with someone?* So what if he had? What he did and who he did it with was his business. Period.

Tossing his jacket onto a wing-backed chair, he crossed his arms over his chest and rocked back on his heels a few times. "And what of it?"

He didn't need his PhD to know that was the wrong answer.

Her eyes cut into him like glass and she took a step toward him.

"Did you not bring me here, Adrian?"

He shrugged a massive shoulder. "Yes, I brought you here with the intent of you getting uninterrupted sleep. What does that have to do with how I spent my time this evening and with whom?"

He wasn't used to this form of inquisition, especially after having spent the past several years making sure no woman assumed she had the right to make any demands on his time. The last time he'd looked, his marital status was still *single*.

"The only reason I brought it up is because you agreed to the pretend affair with me. And in doing so you indicated you would forgo dating for a while," she said.

"And I have."

"Then what about tonight?" she asked brusquely.

He stared at her. "Why the questions, Trinity? Are you jealous or something?"

He could tell from her expression that his question hit a nerve…as well as exposed a revelation. She *was* jealous. He inwardly smiled at that. It looked as if he wasn't the only one plagued with emotions.

"Of course I'm not jealous," she said, dropping her hands from her waist. "I just thought we had an agreement, that's all."

"And we do. Like I said, I wanted you to get uninter- rupted sleep, so after my business dinner, I called Bailey and invited her to a movie."

"Bailey?"

"Yes. My sister Bailey."

"Oh."

"That's all you have to say?" he asked, deciding not to let her off so easily.

"Yes, that's all I have to say…other than I'll be ready to go home when my clothes finish drying, which shouldn't be too long. I'll check on them now." She turned to head toward the laundry room, but he reached out and snagged her arm. He tried ignoring the spike of heat that rushed through him the moment he touched her, but it was obvious that she felt it, as well. "Hey, wait a minute. You owe me an apology."

She lifted her chin. "Do I?"

"What do you think? You all but accused me of lying to you. It was an unnecessary hit to my character and I feel wounded."

Trinity rolled her eyes. "Getting a little carried away, aren't you?"

If only she knew just how carried away he felt. Every cell in his body was sizzling, all the way to the groin. Especially the groin. Desire throbbed all through him, and an urgency he'd never felt before began overtaking his senses. Pushing him on. That had to be the reason he was still holding on to her arm. Something she noticed.

"Why are you touching me, Adrian?"

She was visibly annoyed and visibly turned on. He could see both in her eyes. There were frissons of heat in the dark depths staring back at him. He'd been involved with enough women to know when sexual hunger was coiling inside them. Some women tried ignoring it, pretending they didn't feel a thing. Calling Trinity out on it would only increase her anger.

"You had no right to question me just now," he said, speaking firmly, not liking the way she was making him feel. Or the way he'd been feeling all day while thinking of her.

"You're right. I didn't. But that's not giving me an answer as to why you're touching me."

No, it didn't. If she wanted an answer he would give her one. "I like touching you. I also like kissing you." He saw the way heat flared even more in her gaze, and his body pounded in response.

Then, although he knew she wouldn't like it, he added, "Probably as much as you like kissing me back."

She pulled away from his hold. "Only in your dreams."

He smiled. "Trust me, baby, you don't want to go there. You couldn't handle knowing what my dreams are like."

"I don't want to know," she said, giving him a chagrined look before walking off. Adrian was right on her heels. "About that apology, Trinity."

She turned around so suddenly, she collided with his chest. His arms were on her again, this time to steady her and keep her from falling. And not one to miss any opportunity, he tightened his hold, leaned in close to her lips and whispered, "Since you won't give me an apology, I guess I'll take this instead."

Then he proceeded to ravage her mouth.

The man was a master at kissing.

The last thing Trinity wanted was for Adrian to know how much she wanted him, wanted this. But for the life of her, she couldn't stop responding to his kiss. She was engaging in the exchange in a way that probably told him everything she didn't want him to know. How was she supposed to deal with these emotions he could arouse in her so easily? How was she supposed to deal with him period?

He fit snugly against her. She felt the outline of his body, every single detail. Especially an erection that was as hard as one could get. It was huge, pressing into her middle as if it had every right to let her know just how much it wanted her. And this kiss…

Lordy, it should be outlawed. Arrested. Made to serve time for indecency. Who did stuff like this with their tongue? Evidently Adrian Westmoreland did. And what he was doing was driving her crazy, pushing her over the edge. Goading her into wanting things she didn't need.

Trinity followed his lead and kissed him back with a craving she felt in places she had forgotten existed.

The kiss made her remember it had been a long time since she'd engaged in any type of sexual activity. There had been that one time in college—when it was over she'd sworn it would be the last time. It had been a waste of good bedsheets. It was obvious Ryan Morgan hadn't known what he was doing any more than she had.

Since then, although she'd dated from time to time, and she'd been attracted to one or two men, there hadn't been anyone who'd impressed her enough to get her in his bed. Plenty had tried; all had failed…especially some of the doctors she'd worked with. She had a rule about not connecting her personal and professional lives since doing so would only result in unnecessary drama. But it seemed Casey Belvedere didn't know how to take no for an answer. He was causing drama anyway.

But then Trinity stopped thinking when Adrian intensified the kiss, sinking deeper inside her mouth like he had every right to do so. He used his tongue to lick her into submission. What was he doing to her? Images flashed in her mind of scandalous things… all the other things he could do with that tongue. She began tingling all over, especially between her legs. When she felt something solid against her back she knew he'd somehow cornered her against the wall.

She heard herself moan and felt a tightening in her chest. Is this how it felt to desire a man to the point of craziness? Where she was tempted to tear off his clothes and go at it with no control? And all from a little kiss. Well, she had to admit there was nothing little about it, not when her own tongue was swelling in response, doing things it normally wouldn't do, following his lead. And talk about swelling… The erection pressing against her had thickened and poked hard against her inner thigh.

She instinctively shifted to direct his aim right for the

juncture of her thighs. Ah, it felt so right. Yes, there. He evidently thought so, too, because he began moving his body, grinding against her, holding tight to her hips.

He suddenly broke off and took in a slow breath. She did the same. How long had they gone without breathing? Not long enough, she figured, when he stared hard at her without saying anything. The dampness of his lips said it all. He'd gotten a mouthful and wanted more.

"You taste good, Trinity," he said huskily, reaching up to touch her lower lip with his finger.

Why was she tempted to stick out her tongue and give that finger a slow lick? Or, even worse, suck it into her mouth.

She shook her head hoping to shake off the craziness of that thought. "We've gone too far," she said in a voice she barely recognized as her own.

A seductive smile touched his lips as he used that same finger to slowly caress the area around her mouth, causing shivers to run up her body. "And I don't think we've gone far enough."

He *would* say that, she thought. She shifted her body to move away from him, but he pulled her closer. His body seemed to have gotten harder.

She squared her shoulders, or at least she tried to do so. "Now, look, Adrian—"

"I am looking," he interrupted throatily, while staring at her mouth, "And I like what I see."

The fingers that had moved away from her lips to her chin were warm and soft, long and strong. She needed all the control she could garner. Adrian was making her feel things she'd never felt before. How? Why? She was losing it. That was the only explanation for why she had gone almost eight years without wanting a man and now passion was eating away at her.

"Trinity?"

She lifted her chin, that same chin he was caressing, and held tight to his gaze. "What?" Those long, strong fingers slowly eased to the center of her neck, touching the pulse beating there.

"I do things to you."

If he thought she would admit to that, he was wrong. "Is that what you think?"

He chuckled softly, sensuously. "That's what I know. I can tell."

She was dying to ask how he could tell, but decided to claim denial for as long as she could. "I hate to crush that overblown ego of yours, but you're wrong."

He chuckled again. "Let me prove I'm right, sweetheart."

Trinity pulled back from his touch. She'd had enough of this foolishness. "If you don't mind, I need to get my clothes out of the dryer and get dressed so you can take me to the hospital to get my car."

"Not tonight. It's late." He took a step back and dropped his hands to his sides.

She frowned. If he thought they would share space under the same roof tonight, he needed to think again. "Then I'll call a cab."

"No, you won't. You're staying put until tomorrow. I'll drop you off at the hospital for your car on my way to work in the morning."

And then he had the nerve to walk off. She couldn't believe it. Steaming, she was now the one on his heels. "I can't stay here tonight."

He turned so quickly she almost bumped into him. She caught herself and moved back. He stared at her. "Why not?"

"Because I don't want to. I want to sleep in my own bed."

He crossed his arms over his chest. "And I want you in mine."

She swallowed. "Yours?"

"Yes, you have the guest room all to yourself. And if you need another T-shirt to sleep in, I'll get you one."

Although he hadn't suggested they share the same bed, she was growing angrier by the minute. She told herself it wasn't because he hadn't invited her to be his sleeping partner. That had nothing to do with it. "What I need for you to do is to take me home."

She wished his stance wasn't causing her to check out just how good he looked. Long legs, masculine thighs, slim waist, tight abs. Why did the air in the room suddenly feel electrified? Was that a crackling sound she heard? Why did his eyes look so penetrating, so piercing? Why was she letting him get next to her again?

With a mind of its own her gaze lowered to his crotch. He still had an erection? Lordy! Could a man really get that big and make it last that long?

Her gaze slowly lifted to his eyes. The moment they made eye contact she was snatched into a web of heated desire. What in the world was wrong with her?

"We can't continue to deny we want each other, Trinity. Hell, I don't like it any more than you do," he admitted, grabbing her attention.

She swallowed and went back into denial mode. "What are you talking about?" she asked softly.

He took a step forward, coming to a stop just a few feet in front of her. "I'm talking about the way you're looking at me, the way I'm looking at you. You and I have nothing in common on the outside. But…"

She didn't want to ask but couldn't help doing so. "But what?"

He took another step closer. "But on the inside, it's a different story. Point blank, what I want more than anything is to make you come while screaming my name."

Ten

Adrian believed in saying what he thought and what he felt. He had no qualms stating what he wanted. And he wanted Trinity. He had wanted her from the first time he'd laid eyes on her at Riley's wedding, and when he'd heard she was moving to Denver he'd wanted to put her on his to-do list. But her close association with Thorn had squashed that idea. Everyone knew Thorn was overprotective when it came to people he cared deeply about.

Adrian had heard stories about how Thorn had scared off guys who'd wanted to date his sister Delaney. The other brothers had been just as bad, but Thorn had been the worst. He'd had no problem backing up his threats. And Adrian didn't want to give Thorn any reason to kick his behind, family or no family.

If Adrian knew the score, then why was he willing to skate with danger? Because Trinity, standing there wearing his T-shirt and looking sexier than any woman had a right to look, made him willing to risk it all to find out what she had on beneath that cotton. He wanted her. And when a man wanted a woman, nothing else mattered.

"Scream your name? You've got to be kidding me. No man will get a scream out of me."

Her words made him study her expression. She was actually grinning as if what he'd said was amusing. "Why do you find what I said so far-fetched?"

She rolled her eyes. "I find it more than far-fetched. The notion is so ridiculous it really isn't funny. Don't you know a woman who screams while having sex is just doing it to make her partner think he's doing something when he isn't?"

He leaned back against the side of the sofa table and stared at her, his arms crossed over his chest. "You don't say?"

"Yes," she said as a smile touched her lips. "I'm disappointed. I thought you had more smarts in the bedroom."

He should have been insulted but he wasn't. Instead he was amused, especially at her naïveté. She was wrong and he would just love to prove it. But that was beside the point. He couldn't help wondering why she was convinced she was right.

"I have plenty of bedroom smarts, Trinity. But it seems you've been disappointed along the way by some man who wasn't up to snuff."

She frowned. "It's not just me. It's about women in general. We talk and at times exchange notes, and the comparison is usually the same."

"Really?"

"I wouldn't say it if it wasn't true. I'm a doctor, so I know the workings of the human body. I know about orgasms being a natural way to release sexual buildup. I get that. That's not the problem."

"Then what's the problem?"

"Men, and some women, believing it's all that and a bag of chips when it's more like a stick of gum. When they discover it's not what they heard or what they thought, then they're too embarrassed to admit it was a disappointment. They end up faking it instead of fessing up."

"And you know women who have *faked* it."

"Yes. Can you say with certainty that you don't? Are you absolutely sure that every woman you made scream wasn't doing it to stroke that ego of yours?"

If she was trying to make him doubt his ability in the bedroom, she had a long way to go. "Yes, I can say with one-hundred-percent certainty any screams I helped to generate were the real thing."

She stared at him, probably thinking his conceit had gone to his head.

"Well, believe what you want," Trinity said, rolling her eyes.

"You don't believe me?" he asked, looking at her questioningly.

"No, and before you say it, I have no intention of letting you prove I'm wrong. I'm aware of that particular game men play and don't intend to be a participant."

He couldn't help but smile. "So it's not the orgasm you don't believe in, just the degree of pleasure a woman can feel."

She shrugged her pretty shoulders. "Yes, I guess that's right. I know two people can generate passion, and they can do it to the degree that they lose control. I get that. But what I don't buy is that they can generate passion to the point where they're screaming all over the place while sharing the big O. That's the nonsense that sells romance novels. And I'm a reality kind of girl."

Adrian slowly nodded. *A reality kind of girl.* He was going to enjoy every single minute of proving her wrong, and he would prove her wrong. It wouldn't be a game for him. It would be one of the most serious moments of his life. He would be righting a wrong done to her, whatever had made her think faking it was necessary…and, even worse, that doing so was okay.

He needed time to come up with a plan. "It's late. We

can finish this conversation in the morning, *after* I've had my first cup of coffee. Towels, washcloths, extra toiletries, including an unused toothbrush are beneath the vanity in your bathroom. Good night."

Trinity tried not to stare as Adrian left the room. Sexiness oozed from him with every step he took. He had a walk that made the tips of her nipples hard. Lordy, the man had such a cute tush…. The way his pants fit his backside was a sight to behold. She could imagine her hands clenching each firm and masculine cheek. The fantasy unnerved her. Never before had she focused on any part of a man's anatomy.

Since she wasn't sleepy after having slept most of the day, she decided to stay busy. After folding the clothes she'd taken out of the dryer, she went back into the kitchen. Adrian's housekeeper was good at what she did. Trinity couldn't help looking in the cabinets, impressed at how well stocked and organized things were.

She made a cup of tea and enjoyed the beautiful view of downtown Denver out the living room window. She took a deep breath then sipped her tea, hoping it would stop her heart from pounding. Even when she'd folded clothes and messed around in his kitchen, the erratic pounding in her chest that had started when he'd walked away hadn't stopped. It was as if knowing they were under the same roof and breathing the same air was getting to her. Why?

Trying to put thoughts of him out of her mind she turned back to the view. There was a full moon tonight. Adrian lived in the thick of downtown and the surrounding buildings were massive, the skyscrapers numerous. But he still had a beautiful view of the mountains.

Her own house was on the outskirts of town in the suburbs. Adrian's condo was definitely closer to the hospital. *Adrian.*

Her heart pounded even faster. The nerve of him saying bluntly that he wanted to have sex with her. Just who did he think he was? Maybe pretending to be lovers had gone to his head. Maybe it hadn't been a good idea after all. So far all she'd gotten out of it was Belvedere making her work on her days off out of spite.

That wasn't completely true. Being Adrian's pretend lover had been an eye-opener. It had made her realize how sex-deprived she was. That had to be the reason she was so attracted to him and why he was awakening passion inside of her that she didn't know she had. As she'd told him, she knew orgasms relieved sexual tension, but before meeting him sexual tension was something she hadn't worried about. Sexual urges were foreign to her. Now, with him being so sinfully attractive, her heart was overworked with all the pounding and the lower part of her body constantly throbbed.

"Trinity?"

She gasped at the sound of her name and turned from the window. Adrian stood in his pj bottoms, which rode low on his hips. He looked even sexier than he had earlier that night. "Yes?"

"Why aren't you in bed?"

Seeing him standing there almost took her breath away. And if that wasn't enough, his masculine scent reached out to her, sending her entire body into a heated tailspin, engulfing her with crazy thoughts and ideas. "Why aren't you?" she countered, trying to stay in control.

A slow smile touched his lips and her body tingled in response. That erratic pounding in her chest returned. Had it truly ever left? "I couldn't sleep," was his reply and she watched as he rubbed a hand over his face.

"You need to go back to bed. You work tomorrow. I don't. Besides, thanks to you, I got a lot of rest today."

"No need to thank me. I did what was needed."

He was getting next to her with little or no effort. She glanced down at her cup and came up with the perfect excuse to leave the living room. "Well, I've finished my tea. I guess I'll go to bed now. Maybe more sleep will come."

Her only regret was that she had to walk past him to get to the kitchen. As she walked by he reached out, took the cup from her hand and placed it on the sofa table before wrapping a strong arm around her waist and pulling her to him.

"What do you think you're doing?" she asked, making a feeble attempt to push him away.

"Something I should have done earlier tonight."

She saw his head lowering to hers and opened her mouth to protest. But he seized the opportunity and slid his tongue between her parted lips. Immediately her traitorous tongue latched on to his and before she could fully grasp what was happening, she was kissing him as hungrily as he was kissing her. Never had she wanted or needed a kiss as much as she wanted and needed this one.

Not understanding why, she molded her body to his as if it was the most natural thing, and instinctively wrapped her arms around his neck. She felt those strong, hard fingers on her backside, pressing her closer. She felt him, long, solid and erect against her.

Her brazen response prompted Adrian to deepen the kiss.

Desire felt like talons sinking into her skin, spreading through her body in a heated rush, making her moan deep in her throat. He was the first man to ever make her moan, but she still wasn't buying that screaming claim he'd made earlier.

Then he began grinding against her body. She nearly buckled over; the juncture of her legs felt on fire. She broke off the kiss and unwrapped her arms from his neck before taking in a deep breath. "You don't want this, Trinity. You don't need this. You've got self-control, girl. Use it," she muttered softly under her breath.

Adrian heard her. "What are you saying?" he asked, dipping his head low to hers.

Trinity stared up into penetrating dark eyes. Was he aware that his eyes were an aphrodisiac? Just staring into their dark depths caused crazy things to happen to her. She nervously licked her lips, really tempted to lick his instead.

"Trinity?"

She recalled he had asked her a question. She decided to go for honesty. "I'm trying to talk myself out of taking something that I want but don't need."

He lifted a brow. "Really?"

"Yes."

He placed his hand on her shoulder. "Keep talking. You might convince yourself to walk away, but I have a feeling you won't."

She sucked in a breath. A spark of energy passed between them from his touch, making her fully aware she was being pulled into something hot, raw and sensuous. "You don't think I have any resolve?" she asked him.

"Not saying that. But I know in most cases desire can overrule resolve, no matter what kind of pep talk you give yourself."

She didn't want to agree with him, but unfortunately she was living proof that he might be right. "Why? Why don't I have self-control around you?"

"Maybe you don't need it."

"Oh, I need it," she said. "But..."

"But what?"

"I'm beginning to think I need you more." She paused. "I don't want to make a fool of myself."

"What makes you think you will?"

"Because I'm not good at this."

"Good at what, Trinity?"

"Seduction."

His lips curved into a smile as he reached for her. Those penetrating eyes held hers again as the palm of his hand settled in the center of her back.

"Baby, give me the opportunity and I'll teach you everything you need to know and then some."

I can't mess this up.

That thought raced through Adrian's mind as he dipped his head to capture Trinity's lips. As soon as he was planted firmly inside her mouth he deepened the kiss, ravishing her mouth with a greed that had soaked into his bones. There was no stopping him now. He would sort out what the hell was going on with him later. Much later.

He had tried to come up with a plan for the best way to handle Trinity, but he'd decided a plan would appear too calculating and manipulative. So instead he'd decided to let desire take its course. And it had. He felt it in the way she was kissing him back, letting him know that she was as far gone as he was.

With a mind of their own, his hands moved, traveling from the center of her back to her shoulders before moving lower to cup her shapely backside. She felt good.

When he felt himself harden even more he knew it was time to take things to the next level. He ended the kiss, but kept his hands firmly planted on her backside, making sure their bodies remained connected.

"I want you," he whispered. "I want to take you into my bedroom and make love to you, Trinity."

He saw the indecision in her gaze and knew he had to be totally honest with her. As much as he wanted her, she needed to know where he stood. That was the only way he handled a woman. Trinity would be more than just a quick romp, but he wasn't making any promises of forever. Besides, weeks ago they had already established the fact that they wanted different things out of life.

"Before you answer yea or nay, I just need to reiterate that I'm not the marrying kind," he told her.

He saw the way her eyes widened. "Marry?" she asked in surprise. "Who said anything about marriage?"

"Just saying. Some women expect a lot after a roll beneath the sheets. Just wanted to make sure we're clear that I don't do forever."

"We're clear," she said with one of those matter-of-fact looks on her face. "I guess I should issue that same disclaimer since forever isn't in my future, either."

"Good. We're straight."

And before she could change her mind as to how the night would end for them, he swept her off her feet and into his arms. Quickly headed for the bedroom.

Eleven

Trinity sat cross-legged in the middle of Adrian's bed, where he'd placed her, and watched him slowly ease the pj's down his legs. He was looking at her as if she was a treat he intended to devour. And heaven help her she wanted to devour him, as well.

When he stepped out of his pajama pants, all thoughts left her mind except for one: his engorged manhood. Why did he have to be so well-endowed? No wonder he was conceited and arrogant.

She moved her gaze away from him, figuring that doing so would stop her heart from beating buck-wild in her chest. The décor of his room, like the rest of the house, was fantastic. The dominating colors of avocado and chocolate gave it a manly air. The room was a lot bigger than the guest room she'd been given. At least, it appeared that way since his furniture was positioned to give a very spacious feel.

Adrian walked toward her, completely naked, with that slow and sensual stride that he had down to a tee. Her gaze raked over him and she could imagine touching those tight abs, that muscular chest, those broad shoulders. And that flourishing manhood filled her head with all sorts of ideas.

When he reached the bed and placed a knee on it, she

figured it was time to remind him of what she'd said earlier. "I'm not good at this."

"Let me be the judge of that," he said, reaching for the hem of her T-shirt.

In a blink, he had whipped it over her head, leaving her in black panties and matching bra. But from the way he looked at her one would have thought she wasn't wearing anything at all.

With a flick of his wrist, he unsnapped the front clasp of her bra. Before she could react, he had worked the garment from her shoulders and tossed it aside. Her stomach clenched when she saw his gaze focus on her breasts and the hardened tips of her nipples. His attention made them harder.

She nearly moaned out loud when he licked a swollen nipple then sucked it into his mouth. How had he known doing something like that would make her womanhood weep? She wrapped her hands around his head to hold him to her breast. Was there anything his tongue wasn't capable of doing? She doubted it. It was made to give pleasure. No wonder Adrian was so high in demand. If this was part of his seduction then he could seduce the panties off a nun.

He released one nipple and started on the other. That was when his hand moved lower, easing beneath the waistband of her panties. As if he'd given a silent order, her legs parted to give him better access. It didn't take long for his fingers to find what they were seeking.

She groaned deep in her throat when he slid a finger inside her womanly core, finding her wet. She doubted he expected she'd be otherwise. Then, with the same circular motion his tongue was using, his finger moved likewise inside her, massaging her clitoris. There was no doubt in her mind he was readying for the next phase, but she was already there.

Then he moved his mouth to her lips, swallowing her

groan and thrusting his tongue deep. He kissed her with a hunger that he mimicked with the movement of his finger. At some point he'd added a second finger. Together the two were stroking her into a heated frenzy. Of their own accord, her hips began moving, gyrating to the rhythm of his fingers. She thought she would pass out from the sensations swamping her.

When he finally released her mouth, she gasped, and he took the opportunity to shimmy her panties over her hips and down her legs. Instead of tossing them aside as he'd done with her bra, he lifted them to his nose, inhaling deeply and closing his eyes as if he was enjoying heavenly bliss. Watching him sent sensual chills escalating through her body. She moaned again.

He opened his eyes and tossed the panties aside. He held her gaze as he lowered himself to the juncture of her thighs. And when he licked his lips, she felt her inner muscles clench. It was then that he leaned up and whispered close to her ear, "Last chance to back out."

He had to be kidding. There was no way she would back out, although her common sense was telling her that she should. Instead she'd decided based on feelings, and, at the moment she was dealing with some pretty heady emotions.

"I won't back out."

"If you're certain, now is when I tell you my technique."

"Your technique?" she asked, barely able to get the words out. Surely he wasn't into anything kinky? Although right now, he could come up with just about anything and she would go along with it.

"Yes, my technique. When I make love to you, I'm going to give you all I've got."

She swallowed slowly. "All you've got?"

"Every single inch."

Trinity swallowed again as a vision flashed through

her mind. Her skin burned for him and her womanly core throbbed.

"Ready for me?"

She wasn't sure. All she knew was that when he touched her she felt good. When he kissed her she felt even better. She figured making love to him would be off the charts.

"And, Trinity?"

She looked at him. "Yes?"

"I *will* make you scream and it *will* be the real thing."

Now that he'd given her fair warning, Adrian went about taking care of business. Wrapping his arms around her, he brought them chest to chest. The protruding tips of her nipples poked into him, and he liked the connection.

He eased Trinity onto her back while kissing her, doubting he would ever get tired of tasting her. He loved the way she kissed him, devouring him as much as he devoured her. How could any woman have so much passion and not know it?

He broke off the kiss. When her head touched one pillow, he reached behind her to grab another. Lifting her hips, he placed the pillow beneath her and then used his knee to spread her legs. He licked his lips in anticipation as he gazed at her wet womanly folds.

Adrian ran a hand up and down her thigh, loving the feel of her naked flesh. She had soft skin and the scent of a woman. She was perfectly made. He'd thought so when he'd seen her in clothes and he thought so even now that he'd seen her out of them.

"Adrian?"

He met her gaze and saw impatience. He wouldn't be rushed. If she thought he was one of those be-done-with-it kind of guys, she was mistaken. When it came to sex, he was so painstakingly thorough it was almost a shame. Before the night was over, she would discover just how wrong she was about the sexual experience for a woman. No woman left Adrian Westmoreland's bed unsatisfied; he made sure of it.

And Trinity was a special case because he could tell from their conversations that she had limited experience in the bedroom. He intended to remedy that. Tonight.

He kissed her, letting his tongue mimic what his manhood intended to do once he was inside her. But first, one taste led to another. Her scent was driving him insane.

Adrian moved his hands all over her body, loving to touch her. He trailed kisses from her mouth to the center of her throat. He sucked her, intentionally branding her. He wasn't sure why, especially when he didn't believe in giving a woman any ideas regarding possession. But for Trinity, it was necessary.

Needing to touch her again, he ran a hand over her breasts and stomach before moving lower, to her thighs, brushing his fingertips over her flesh and loving the softness of her silky-smooth skin. And he loved watching her nipples harden in front of his eyes, loved seeing her light brown eyes darken and stare back at him filled with a heated lust that mirrored his own.

"I want you bad," he muttered, putting into words just how he felt. His mouth moved from her neck back up to her lips. Down below, his fingers slid back between her legs. There was something about touching her there that he found exhilarating. And he liked the way her legs spread open of their own accord. When he stroked her nub, she threw her head back and moaned. He loved the sound and wanted to hear more.

He licked her lips, wanting more of her taste. Now. He eased his body downward to lower his head between her legs. When his tongue slid between the slippery wet folds of her womanhood, she moved against his mouth.

When it came to oral sex he was a master, and he was

about to show Trinity just what a pro he was. Doing so would be easy because she tasted so damn good.

He heard her release a deep groan and he smiled. She hadn't felt anything yet. He was just getting started. In a few more minutes she would be pulling his hair. With a meticulousness he had perfected over the years, Adrian devoured Trinity's sweetness, moving his tongue inside her from every angle.

Her legs began to quiver against the sides of his face. She dug into his scalp while bringing her hips off the pillow. But what he wanted to hear more than anything were her luscious whimpers that escalated into a full-blown moan.

She was trying to hold in what she was feeling. He wasn't having any of that. He knew the sound he wanted to hear and decided to use his *deep tongue* technique on her. Within seconds, her moans became screams. He held her as she jerked, an orgasm sweeping through her. It might have started between her legs but he could tell from the intensity of her scream that she'd felt it through her entire body.

He didn't let up. Another scream arrived on the heels of the last and it was only when she finally slumped back against the pillow that he lifted his head. Leaning back on his haunches, he looked at her. Her hands were thrown over her eyes and her breathing sounded as if she'd run a marathon.

When she sensed him staring at her, she dropped her hand and stared back.

He smiled, licked his lips and asked, "Was that the real thing or were you faking it?"

Trinity wasn't sure she was capable of answering. Her throat felt raw from her screams. Never in her life had she experienced anything quite like what Adrian had just done to her. The man's mouth, his tongue, should be outlawed.

She had screamed—actually screamed—and there hadn't been anything fake about.

"Still not sure? Then I better step up my game."

He had to be kidding. But when he shifted his body, she saw that he wasn't. His bigger-than-life manhood stood at full attention.

"Adrian," she whispered. He reached into the nightstand to pull out a condom packet. She swallowed, moistening her lips while watching him put it on. How could a woman get turned on by that? Easily, she thought, seeing how expertly he shielded himself. Thick, protruding veins ran along the sides of his erection and the head was engorged. An eager shiver raced through her.

He reached for her and she went to him willingly, not caring that he could probably see the desire all over her face. "We start off doing traditional and then we get buck wild," he murmured against her lips.

He tilted her hips toward him and entered her, inch by slow inch. She closed her eyes in sexual bliss. Her body felt tight even as it adjusted to the size of him. He stretched her, lodging himself deep, to the hilt.

"You okay, baby?"

Trinity's fingernails dug into his shoulders and she inhaled a deep breath. He had gone still, but she could feel him throbbing inside her. She held tight to his gaze as a tremor ran through her. She could tell from the look in his eyes that he felt it. He got harder, bigger.

And then he began to move. If she thought his tongue needed to be outlawed, then his manhood needed to be put in jail and the key thrown away. Something inside her ignited. He thrust in and out, going deeper. She felt him, every hard inch, with each slow, purposeful stroke.

Emotions she'd never felt before raced through her. Instinctively, her hips moved, mimicking his. Sensations overwhelmed her as he continued to pump, going fast and then slow and then fast all over again.

Something started at her womb, spreading through every part of her. Her legs began to tremble; a sound erupted at the base of her throat.

He was hitting her G spot, H spot, Q spot—every spot inside her—driving her closer to the edge with every thrust. He pumped harder, longer, the intensity of his strokes triggering hot, rolling, mind-blowing feelings.

And then the world seemed to spin out of control. An orgasm tore through her. She screamed, louder than before. Waves of ecstasy nearly drowned her in pleasure. She screamed again. This time she screamed out his name. As if the sound propelled him, he thrust inside her as another climax claimed her. Then his body bucked hard and she heard her name on his lips.

Moments later, he slumped against her and then shifted their bodies so she was on top of him. He gently rubbed his hand up and down her back. "You screamed my name," he rasped huskily.

"And you screamed mine." She raised her head from his chest to point that out.

A crooked smile touched the corners of his mouth. "So I did." He didn't say anything for a long moment. "I asked you before, Trinity. Were your screams the real thing?"

She wished she could lie and say they weren't, but to do so wouldn't serve any purpose. He had proved her wrong in the most shocking yet delicious manner. It was a lesson she doubted she would ever forget.

"Yes," she whispered softly. "They were the real thing." She placed her head back down on his chest.

She should not have been surprised about his vast knowledge of ways to pleasure a woman, but she couldn't help wondering how many women he'd been involved with to obtain that experience.

"Tired?"

She lifted her head again. "Exhausted."

In one smooth movement he shifted his body and had her on her back again so he could stare down at her. "Then I guess this time I'll do all the work."

This time? She stared at him. Surely he didn't have another round of sex on his mind. Evidently he did, she thought, watching him grab another condom from the nightstand drawer. "Time to swap out," he said, smiling at her.

He eased off the bed and trotted naked toward the bathroom. Lordy, the man had the kind of butt cheeks that made her want to rub against them all day and all night. The kind that tempted her to pinch them for pleasure.

"You can do whatever you like," he said, turning around and grinning at her.

Jeez. Did he have eyes in the back of his head? Or was he a mind reader? "I have no idea what you're talking about."

He chuckled.

"Don't let me prove you wrong again, Trinity."

Then, after winking at her, he went into the bathroom and closed the door behind him.

Twelve

Before daybreak Adrian had proved Trinity wrong in more ways and positions than she'd known existed. He'd made love to her through most of the night, guiding her through one mind-blowing orgasm after another.

Although she was one hell of a passionate woman, her sexual experience was limited. He had no problems teaching her a few things. He couldn't recall ever enjoying making love to any woman more. It had been an incredible night, which was why he was awake and had been since four that morning.

His heart was still pounding from when she had gone down on him. The first time she'd ever done so with any man, she had admitted. He had felt honored. He had no problem telling her what he liked and she had readily complied. Whether she knew it or not, she had a mouth that was made for more than just kissing.

He glanced over at her, naked and curled beside him with her leg tossed over his. She was luscious temptation, even asleep. It wouldn't take much for him to shift a little and ease inside her.

Without a condom? He blinked. What the hell was he thinking? He'd never even imagined making love to

a woman without wearing protection, regardless of what
form of protection she was using. That wasn't Adrian Westmoreland's way. But it also wasn't his way to let a woman
spend the night at his place, either. For any reason. However, she had. And why did it look as if she belonged here,
naked in his bed beside him?

Not liking the direction of his thoughts, he gently detan-
gled her leg from his before quietly easing out of the bed.
While sliding into his pj bottoms he glanced over at her.
Immediately, he got hard. Trinity was too damn desirable
for her own good. After making love to her, she had become
an itch he wanted to scratch again and again.

Closing the bedroom door behind him, he took the stairs
two at a time. He needed a drink, something highly intox-
icating. But because tomorrow was a workday, he would
settle for a beer instead. And he needed to talk to someone.
The two people he could relate to the most were Aidan, his
twin, and his cousin Bane.

Aidan was probably asleep and no telling what Bane
was up to. Last time they'd talked, Bane was leaving for
an assignment and couldn't say where. Adrian had a feeling Bane was enjoying being a navy SEAL.

He tried Bane's number, but when he didn't get an answer, he dialed Aidan. A groggy Aidan answered on the
fourth ring. "Dr. Westmoreland."

"Wake up. We need to talk."

It took a while for Aidan to respond. "Why?"

"It's Trinity."

Adrian heard a yawn, followed by yet another one-word
question. "And?"

Adrian rubbed a hand down his face. "And I might have
gone beyond my boundaries."

There was another pause. This one just as long as the
last. "I told you I felt your emotions and they were strong.
What did you expect, Adrian?"

"Damn it, Aidan. I expected to have more control, and not to forget Thorn is her brother-in-law. He thinks of her as a sister. Tonight I've been only thinking of one thing." *To get more of her.*

"Now that your common sense has returned, what do you plan to do?"

Adrian sucked in a deep breath. He wasn't at all sure his common sense had returned. What he should be doing was hiking back upstairs, waking Trinity to tell her to get dressed so he could take her to the hospital to get her car. Then, if he really had any sense, he would tell her that pretending to be lovers wasn't working and that she should come up with another plan to get Belvedere off her back. However, he could do none of those things.

"Adrian?"

"Yes?" He took a huge sip of his beer.

"So what do you plan to do?"

Adrian wiped the back of his hand across his lips. "Not what I should be doing." He placed the half-empty beer bottle on the counter. "It's late. Sorry I bothered you."

"It's early and no bother. Just don't get yourself into any trouble. I'm not there to bail you out if you do."

Adrian couldn't help but smile. "Like you ever did. If I recall correctly, most of the time whenever I got in trouble it was because of you, Bane or Bailey."

"All right, if that's what you want to believe."

"That's what I remember."

"Whatever, Adrian. Good night"

Adrian still held the phone in his hand long moments after he'd heard his twin click off the line. He knew Aidan was dealing with his own issues with Jillian, and Adrian pitied him. He wouldn't want to be in his brother's shoes when Dillon and Pam found out Aidan had been messing around with one of Pam's sisters. Everyone knew how protective Pam was of her three sisters.

Probably the same way Tara is of hers.

Adrian picked up his beer bottle and took another swig. He didn't want to think about overprotective sisters tonight. But then, what he did want to think about was liable to get him in trouble.

Going back to bed was out of the question. Since he wasn't sleepy, he went into his office to get a jump start on the day's work. In addition to the mall complex on Amelia Island, they were looking at building another hotel and mall in Dallas.

In other words, he had too many things on his plate to be standing in his kitchen at four in the morning, remembering how great it felt being between Trinity's luscious pair of legs.

Sunlight hit Trinity in the face. She snatched open her eyes. Glancing around the room she remembered in vivid detail what had happened in this bed.

She moved and immediately felt soreness in her inner muscles, reminding her of the intensity of the lovemaking she and Adrian had shared. And she had screamed. More than once. The look on his face had been irritatingly smug. Too darn arrogant and self-satisfied to suit her.

And speaking of conceited eye candy, where was he? Why was she in his bed alone? Flashes of what had gone down last night kept passing through her mind. Actually, *she* had gone down.

She vividly recalled taking the thick, throbbing length of him in her hand, marveling at its size, shape and hardness, fascinated by the thick bulging veins. She had leaned down to kiss it, but once her lips were there, she had opened her mouth wide and taken him inside. That was the first time she'd done such a thing and now the memories set every nerve ending inside her body on fire.

A sound from downstairs cut into her thoughts. Was that

the shower running in one of the guest bedrooms down-stairs? It was still early, not even six o'clock. Why was Adrian using the shower downstairs instead of the one he had in his master bath?

A part of her figured she should stay put and wait until he returned to the room. But another part—the bold side she'd discovered last night—wanted to see him now.

Refusing to question what was going through her mind, she eased out of bed. Looking around for her T-shirt, she found it tossed over a chair. Slipping it over her head, she opened the door and proceeded down the stairs, following the sound of the shower.

She opened the guest bedroom door. It was just as nice as the room she'd used. Nerves made her hesitate when she reached the bathroom door, but she didn't announce her presence. Instead she pushed the door open and stepped inside.

Adrian stood inside the shower stall as jets of water gushed over his naked body. She placed her hand to her throat. *Oh, my.* Water ran from his close-cropped hair to broad shoulders, a powerful chest and muscular legs. The area between her own legs throbbed just like the night be-fore. Maybe worse.

She leaned back against the vanity, and continued to stare at him. She might as well get an eyeful since he hadn't detected her presence yet. His back was to her and those masculine wet butt cheeks were definitely worth ogling. She couldn't help but appreciate how they clenched and tightened whenever he raised his hands to wash under his arms.

For crying out loud, when did I begin drooling over any man's body?

Even as she asked herself that question, she knew she'd never drooled over anyone until Adrian.

He must have heard a sound—probably the pounding in

her chest—because he turned around. The moment their gazes locked, a surge of sexual energy jolted her.

He opened the shower door. With water dripping from his body, he said, "Join me."

Need spread through her as she moved toward the shower stall, pausing briefly to whip the T-shirt over her head and toss it aside.

The moment she stepped into the shower, he joined her mouth with his, burying his long, strong fingers into her hair. Water washed over them. Closing her eyes, she sighed when the taste of his tongue met with hers. Awareness of him touched every pore of her body. Her desire for him was burning her to the core.

He let go of her hair, his hands cupping her face as he kissed her as though his very life depended on it. The kiss was everything she'd come to expect from him—dominating, powerful and methodically thorough.

He dropped his hands from her face and wrapped strong arms around her, bringing her wet body closer to his as water rained down on them. He ended the kiss then reached behind him to grab the soap and begin lathering both their bodies. He ran his hands up her arms, around her back and gave special attention to her buttocks and thighs. Her heart rate escalated with every glide of his hands.

Then he lifted her and pressed her back against the marble wall.

"Wrap your legs around me."

Automatically she obeyed, feeling his hard length against her stomach. He tilted her body, widening the opening of her legs, and in one smooth sweep, slid inside her. She felt every inch of him as he drove into her deeper.

Warm water sprayed down as he pumped hard and fast. She clung to him, digging her fingernails into his back. Her body wanted even more. Somehow Adrian knew it, and he gave it to her. His hand slid under her bottom, touching the spot he wanted, right where their bodies were joined. He stroked her there.

She couldn't take any more. She sank her teeth into his shoulder. Her action drove him on, unleashing the erotic beast in him. He released a deep, throaty groan that triggered a response inside her.

She screamed his name, then sobbed when spasms took her deeper into sexual paradise. The magnitude of the pleasure made her scream again.

And even with water pouring down on them, she felt him spill inside her. Hot, molten liquid flooded her, messing with her senses and jumbling her sanity.

She met his gaze. "More."

That single word pushed him, making him hard all over again. The feel of him stretching her even more than before had her thighs and backside trembling.

Then he moved again, going in and out of her in quick, even thrusts, a sinfully erotic hammering of his hips. He stared down at her, the intensity and desire that filled his eyes more torture than she could bear.

"Adrian."

She murmured his name in a heated rush just before a powerful force rammed through her. She felt each and every sensation, the next more powerful than the last. She bit into Adrian's shoulder to keep from screaming and arched her back to feel it all.

He tossed his head back and called out her name, exploding inside her yet again. He cupped her buttocks and kept coming, giving her the *more* she wanted, what she'd demanded.

"Satisfied?" he asked against her wet lips.

Even after all of that, desire for him was still thick in her blood.

She placed a kiss on his lips as a jolt of sexual pleasure rocked her to the bone. She couldn't help but smile, and then she whispered, "Very much so."

Thirteen

"Didn't you get any sleep last night, Adrian?" Stern Westmoreland asked with a grin. "We expect you to start snoring at any minute."

Adrian blinked. Had he been caught dozing off during a meeting? He glanced around the room and saw the silly grins on the faces of his cousins Riley and Canyon, and a rather concerned look on Dillon's features. Adrian sat straighter in his chair. "Yes, I got plenty of sleep," he lied.

"Oh, then we must be boring you," Canyon observed, chuckling.

Dillon stood as he closed the folder in front of him. "I've caught the three of you snoozing a time or two, so leave him be."

Adrian knew Dillon's words were to be obeyed…for now. But he knew his cousins well enough to know that he hadn't gotten the last of the ribbing from them. He stood to leave with Dillon. He wouldn't dare stay behind and tangle with the three jokesters.

Dillon glanced over at him as they headed down the corridor to their respective offices. "So, how is that situation going with Trinity?"

If only Dillon really knew, Adrian thought, the muscles of his manhood throbbing at the memory. He'd had the time of his life last night and wouldn't be surprised if he really had been dozing during the meeting. He'd gotten little sleep, but the sex had been off the charts. He would even go on record as saying it had been the best he'd ever had. And just to think, she was still practically an amateur.

But he intended to remedy that. Last night might have been their first time between the sheets, but it wouldn't be their last. He wasn't sure how Trinity felt about it, though. She hadn't had much to say this morning during the drive over to the hospital to get her car. In fact, she had taken the time to get more sleep. He'd left her alone, figuring she needed it.

Before he could ask when they could get together again, she had muttered a hasty, "See you later," and had quickly gotten out of his car and into hers. There hadn't been a goodbye kiss or anything.

"Adrian?"

The sound of Dillon's voice cut into his thoughts. "Yes?"

"I asked how that situation is going with Trinity."

"Fine." He tried to ignore the scrutinizing gaze his cousin was giving him.

"And how did things work out a few days ago when Dr. Belvedere requested that she work on her days off?"

Anger flashed in Adrian's eyes. "It was just as I suspected. According to Trinity, Belvedere came on to her again, even mentioned the night he'd seen us out together. He told her to drop me or else."

Adrian saw a mirror image of his own anger in Dillon's eyes. "Did she report it?"

"Yes, but the chief of pediatrics accused her of exaggerating, causing unnecessary drama." Adrian paused. "I met Belvedere face-to-face."

Dillon lifted a brow. "When?"

"Knowing how tired she would be I decided to pick

Trinity up from work yesterday morning. And wouldn't you know it, he was there in her face, insinuating he would be picking her up for a date that night, after having made her work on her days off. It didn't occur to him that she might need to rest."

"What did you do?"

"Not what I wanted to do, Dil, trust me. You should have seen her. She was so exhausted she could barely stand. With self-control you would have been proud of, I introduced myself to Dr. Belvedere as her significant other and told him that Trinity had other plans for the evening. Then we left. I drove her to my place instead of taking her home. I figured Belvedere would be crazy enough to drop by her home, regardless of what I'd told him. Besides, I wanted to make sure she got uninterrupted sleep."

Dillon nodded. "Did she?"

"Yes. She slept all day while I was at work, and it was late when I got in last night after that dinner meeting with Kenneth Jenkins and a movie date with Bailey. But when I got home I could see that she'd gotten plenty of rest."

Dillon nodded again. "Then you took her home?" he asked, giving Adrian another scrutinizing gaze. It took everything Adrian had not to squirm beneath his cousin's intense examination.

"No. It was late, so she stayed the night."

"Oh, I see."

Adrian had a feeling Dillon was beginning to see too much and decided now was the time to make a hasty exit. "Well, I'll check with you later. I have that Potter report to finalize for Canyon."

He quickly walked off but stopped when Dillon called out to him. "Adrian?"

He turned around. "Yes?"

"Will you be available for tomorrow's chow-down?"

Adrian shrugged. "I'm free tomorrow night so there's no reason I won't be there."

Dillon smiled. "Good. It's JoJo's birthday and although she doesn't want to make it a big deal, you know Pam, she will make it a big deal anyway."

"Then I'll make it my business to be there."

"You can invite Trinity to join us if you like."

Adrian stared at his cousin. "Why would I like?"

"No special reason—just a suggestion. Besides, it might be a good idea to give the family an update. If Belvedere keeps it up, we might have to present a show of unity. The Westmorelands have just as much name recognition in this town as the Belvederes."

Adrian nodded. "Okay. I'll give it some thought."

He walked away giving it a lot of thought. Trinity was no longer a pretend lover. Last night he'd made her the real thing.

Trinity sat at her kitchen table finishing her dinner with a cup of hot tea. After Adrian had dropped her off at the hospital for her car, she had driven home, shivered and gone straight to bed. She'd appreciated her second day of nonstop sleep and inwardly admitted she'd been nearly as tired this morning as she had been the day before. Just for a different reason.

She had spent most of last night making love with Adrian. Now it was late afternoon and other than sleeping, she hadn't gotten anything done. Definitely not the laundry she'd planned to do today. Instead she had mentally berated herself for her brazen behavior last night. Who begs a man to ejaculate inside her, for Pete's sake? She cringed each and every time she remembered what she'd said and how he'd complied.

But while her mind was giving her a rough time about it, her body was trembling at the memory. All she had to do was close her eyes to remember how he'd felt inside her—stretching her, pounding into her then exploding inside her.

That's what she kept remembering more than anything. The feel of him exploding. He'd gotten harder, thicker... and then *wham!* His hot release had scorched, triggering her own orgasm.

She tightened her legs together when an ache of smoldering desire pooled right there.

What in the world is wrong with me? she asked herself. *I go without sex for years and then the first time I get a little action I go crazy.*

She took a deep breath, knowing it was more than just getting a little action. More than getting a *lot* of action. She was reacting to becoming involved with a man who knew what to do with what he had. Buffed, toned, sexy to a degree that couldn't even be defined, and on top of that, he knew how to deliver pleasure to the point that he'd made her scream. Lordy, she had screamed her lungs out like a banshee. It's a wonder none of his neighbors had called the police.

To think they had gotten careless and engaged in unprotected sex. Luckily she was on the pill and he had seemed quite relieved about that fact when she had told him later that night. He told her that making love to a woman without using a condom was unlike him. His only excuse was that he had lost control in the moment. She understood because so had she. Once it was established that they were both in good health, he hadn't used a condom for the rest of the night.

She stood now and gathered her dishes to place them in the sink. Then why, after behaving in a way so unbecoming, were her fingers itching to call his number, hear his voice, suggest that he come over?

She shook her head, inwardly chiding herself for letting a man get next to her to this magnitude. Besides, she had to work tomorrow and the last thing she needed was another night filled with sex.

Later she had washed the dishes, cleaned up the kitchen and tackled the laundry when there was a knock at her door. It could have been anyone but the way her body responded signaled it had to be one particular person. Adrian.

She could pretend she wasn't at home but that wouldn't stop the way her heart was beating. Only Adrian had this kind of effect on her and it annoyed her that he knew it.

She crossed the room to the door. "Who is it?" As if she didn't know.

"Adrian."

Why did he always have to sound so good?

"What do you want?"

"Do you really have to ask me that?"

Her heart skipped a beat. How on earth had she gone from a woman who didn't date to a woman who'd made a man's booty-call list? Annoyed by the very thought, she unlocked the door and snatched it open.

She also opened her mouth to give him the dressing down he deserved when suddenly that same mouth was captured by his.

This, Adrian thought as he deepened the kiss, was what he'd been thinking about all day....

She returned the kiss with the same fierce hunger he felt. It was hard to tell whose tongue was doing the most work. Did it matter when the result was so damn gratifying?

He pulled back, ending the kiss. It was either that or take her right there at her front door. A vision of doing just that immediately popped into his mind. Damn, he had it bad.

"You coming here wasn't a good idea."

"I happen to think the opposite," he said, maneuvering past her.

"Hey, wait. I didn't invite you in."

He smiled. "No, but your scent did."

She rolled her eyes as she closed the door. "My scent? What does that have to do with anything?"

He chuckled. "I'll tell you later. This is for now," he said, holding up a bag from a well-known Chinese chain. "I brought dinner."

She crossed her arms over her chest. "Thanks, but I've eaten."

"I haven't. Join me at the table. Besides, we need to talk."

Trinity stared at him and nodded. "Yes, we do need to talk."

She led him to the kitchen and he followed, appreciating the sway of her shapely hips in the cute little skirt she was wearing. He remembered how those same hips had ridden him hard last night.

And then he was drinking up her scent—a scent he remembered from last night. The scent of a woman who wanted a man—and he would admit he was just that arrogant to assume the man was him.

She took a seat at the table while he moved around her kitchen as though he'd spent time in it before. He opened cabinets and pulled out whatever he needed for his meal. From the look on her face he could tell she wasn't thrilled.

"Sure you don't want any?" he asked, emptying the contents of the carton into a bowl. When she didn't respond he glanced over his shoulder and met her gaze. He'd gained the ability to read her well and he smiled when he recalled what he had asked her. The desire in her gaze was her undoing. "I was asking if you want any of *my food,* Trinity. Not if you want any of me. Besides, I already know that you do."

"I do what?"

"Want me."

She stood and narrowed her gaze at him. "You've got a lot of nerve saying something like that."

"Then call me a liar. But be forewarned, if you do, I'll make sure before leaving here to prove I'm right."

Trinity gnawed on her bottom lip. More than anything she would like to call him a liar but knew she couldn't.

Sighing dismissively, she studied the man standing in the middle of her kitchen as if he had every right to be there. It was obvious he had dropped by his place to change clothes. Gone was the designer suit he'd worn that morning. Now he wore a pair of jeans and a V-necked sweater. Blue. Her favorite color. No matter how much she fought her drumming heart, she couldn't get a handle on it.

"Don't look at me like that, baby."

His words made her blink. It was then that she realized just how she'd been looking at him. She glanced away for a moment and then back at him. "I think last night might have given you the wrong idea."

He chuckled. "You think?" he asked, opening her refrigerator.

"I'm serious, Adrian."

"So am I," he said, turning back to her with a bottle of water in his hand. "To be honest, you didn't give me any ideas but you gave me a drowsy day. I dozed a few times in a meeting with my cousins."

Trinity could certainly understand that happening. She shrugged as she sat down. "It wasn't my fault."

"No, it wasn't your fault," he said, coming over to join her at the table with his bowl and bottle of water. "It was mine. I couldn't get enough of you."

She gave him time to sit and say grace, while her mind reeled. Did he have to say exactly whatever he thought? "Well, regardless, no matter how much you couldn't get enough, I think we need to agree here and now that what happened last night was—"

"Don't you dare say a mistake," he said, before opening the water bottle to take a sip.

"What do you want to call it?"

"A night to remember," he said huskily, taking her hand in his.

The instant he touched her, she felt it; the same sensations she'd felt last night. The same ones that had gotten her into trouble. Slowly she pulled her hand from his and looked at him pointedly. "A night we both should forget."

"Don't count on that happening." And then he changed the subject. "So how was your day?" He slid the water bottle he'd taken a drink from just moments ago over to her. "Take a sip. You look hot and it might cool you off."

Fourteen

The next move was hers, Adrian thought, holding Trinity's gaze.

She was obviously a mass of confusion, saying one thing and meaning another. He knew the feeling. He had walked around the office all day thinking he had gotten carried away last night. Nothing could have been *that* good. But by the time he'd left the office and gone home, he'd admitted the truth to himself. Of all the lovers he'd ever had, Trinity took the cake. Last night had been simply amazing. The best he'd ever had. For a man who'd had his share of lovers since the age of fifteen, that was saying a lot.

Now, since arriving on her doorstep, she had tried to make him think she hadn't enjoyed the night as much as he had. He'd listened and now it was time for action. First, he'd help her acknowledge the truth, which meant admitting they had a thing for each other. And it wasn't going anywhere.

"I don't need a drink to cool off. I'm not hot."

So she was still in denial. "You sure?" he asked, holding her gaze intently.

"What I'm sure about, Adrian, is that our little farce has

gone too far. We were supposed to only pretend something was going on between us."

"And what's wrong with making it the real thing?"

"Plenty. I don't have time to get involved in a relationship, serious or otherwise. My career is in medicine. It is my life. I told you my goal. I'm leaving here. I don't do large cities. I want to return to Bunnell and nobody is going to make me change my plans."

Adrian was thinking she had it all wrong, especially if she assumed he was looking for something permanent. He wasn't. But then, what was he looking for? A part-time bed partner? An affair that was destined to go nowhere? Both were his usual method of operation so why did those options bother him when it came to her?

"I don't want to be a booty call for any man, Adrian."

Now Adrian was confused. She didn't want an exclusive relationship nor did she want a casual one, either. "Then what do you want, Trinity? You can't have it both ways."

She lifted her chin. "Can't I be satisfied with having neither?"

The answer to that was simple. "No. Because you're a very hot-blooded woman. You have more passion in your little finger than some women have in their entire bodies. I can say that because I was fortunate enough to tap into all that fire last night. The results were overwhelming. And now that I have tapped into it, for you to go back to your docile life won't be easy. It's like a sexual being has been unleashed and once unleashed, there's no going back."

He paused, finishing the last of his meal and then pushing the bowl aside. "So what are you going to do about it, Trinity? Are you going to drive yourself crazy and try to ignore the passionate person that you are? Or will you accept who and what you are and enjoy life…no matter where it takes you? It's your life to do with it whatever you want, for as long as you want. So do it."

Adrian could see her mind dissecting what he'd said. He didn't know what her decision would be. He could see she was fighting a battle of some sort within her. For the past few years she had been so focused on her medical career that the idea of shifting her time and attention to anything or anyone else was probably mind-boggling to her. But as he'd told her, after last night there was no way she could go back.

They didn't say anything for a long moment. They merely sat staring at each other. He was certain she was feeling the sexual tension building between them. The desire in her eyes was unmistakable. It made his already hard body harder. But whatever she chose had to be her decision.

Minutes ticked by. Then, as he watched, she picked up the bottle of water and slowly licked the rim of the opening—the same place his mouth had touched earlier—before taking a sip. Then she placed the bottle down and licked her own lips as if she'd not only enjoyed the water but the taste of him left behind.

His stomach clenched. The pounding pulse in his crotch was almost unbearable. She had made her decision.

Yearning surged through his every pore and coiling arousal thickened his groin.

When the desire to have her became too strong, he pushed back in his chair and patted his lap, making his erection obvious.

"Come and sit right here."

Trinity felt the pooling of moisture between her legs. It was the way he was looking at her, was the way his huge arousal pressed against the zipper of his jeans. And he wanted her to sit on it? Seriously?

Her gaze slowly moved back to his eyes. She knew he intended for her to do more than just sit. She'd discovered last night that when it came to sex, the man came up with ideas that were so ingenuously erotic they should be patented.

He was right in saying he had tapped into something within her last night, something she hadn't known she possessed. An inner sexual being that he had definitely unleashed.

She would be the first to admit that today, upon waking from her long nap, she had felt the best she'd felt in years. Working off all that stress in the bedroom had its advantages.

So what was she waiting for? As he'd pointed out, it was her life. She could do whatever she wanted, and what she wanted at the moment was *that,* she thought, shifting her gaze back to his groin.

Pushing her chair back, she stood and while still holding his gaze released the side hook of her skirt and shimmied out of it. The look of surprise in his eyes was priceless. She fought back a smile. Did he think he was the only one who could go after what he wanted once his mind was made up?

"You look good."

A smile touched her lips. Evidently, he had no problem with her standing in her kitchen wearing only a tank top and a thong. As if not to be outdone, he stood, kicked aside his shoes, unbuckled his belt and relieved himself of his jeans.

Lordy, was it possible for him to have gotten even bigger since this morning? Her expression must have given away her thoughts because he said, "It's just your imagination."

She frowned, not liking that he knew what she was thinking.

"But why take my word for it? You can always check it out for yourself," he added.

She lifted her chin. "I intend to do just that."

Boldly, she walked over to him and cupped him. He felt engorged, thick, hard. Deciding the outside wasn't telling

her everything, she fished her hand beneath the waistband
of his briefs.

Oh-h, this was it. She brazenly stroked him. She needed
the full length so she shoved his briefs down past his knees
and he stepped out of them.

"That's better," she said in a whisper when she had him
gripped in her hand once again.

"Is it?"

The throaty catch in his voice was followed by a deep
moan when her fingers stroked the length of him from base
to tip and back again. She met his gaze and saw the fiery
heat embedded in the depths of his eyes. The tips of her
nipples hardened in response. "Yes. And I still think it's
bigger than last night. That's amazing," she said.

"No, you are."

She smiled, appreciating Adrian's compliment. "What's
with all these flattering remarks?"

"I wouldn't say them if you didn't deserve them. I don't
play those kinds of games."

So he said, but as far as she was concerned this was
definitely game playing. There was nothing else to call it.
They weren't having an affair. Not really. And she wasn't
into casual sex. At least not the way most would define
it. To keep things straight in her mind she *had* to think of
what was between them as a game. That would keep her
from getting too serious because with every game there
were rules. And when it came to Adrian Westmoreland
she needed plenty.

First of all, he was a man a woman could give her heart
to, and that wasn't a good thing because he didn't want a
woman's heart. For him, it was all about sex. He didn't have
a problem with that since she was a willing partner with
her own agenda. But she had to make sure she didn't slip
and mistakenly think that since the sex was so good, there
had to be more behind it.

She looked up at him as she continued to intimately caress him. If anyone had told her that one day she would be standing in the middle of her kitchen half naked, stroking the full length of a man's penis, she would not have believed them.

"Enjoying yourself?"

"Yes, I'm enjoying myself. Having the time of my life. How do you feel about now?"

"Horny."

She chuckled. "I have a feeling you were already in that state when you arrived on my doorstep. I'm not crazy, Adrian. You only came here tonight for one thing."

The smile that curved his lips made her fingers grip him even tighter. "Actually, two things," he said.

Before she could ask what that second thing was, in a move so smooth she didn't see it coming, he quickly sat and pulled her onto his lap to straddle him.

He shoved aside her thong and entered her before she could utter any word other than, *"Oh."*

Then it was on. She wasn't sure who was riding whom or who was emanating the most heat. All she knew was that her hips were moving in ways they had never moved before, settling on his length and then raising up just enough to make him growl before lowering again. Over and over. Deeper and deeper. Fast and then slow.

She managed to lean in and kiss the corners of his lips, and then she used the tip of her tongue to lick around his mouth. She got the response she wanted when he grabbed her and thrust deeper.

Then it seemed the chair was lifted from the floor as he began pounding harder and harder into her. He froze, holding his position deep inside her. Her inner muscles clenched him, squeezing him tight. That's when he exploded. She felt it, she felt him and then she came, screaming out his name.

He held firm to her hips, keeping their bodies connected

while they shared the moment. She dropped her head to his shoulder and inhaled his scent. She wrapped her arms around him and felt the broad expanse of his muscular back. Perfect. He was as perfect a lover as could be.

Lover...

Is that what he was to her? No longer a pretend lover but the real thing? For how long? Hadn't she told herself just a few hours ago that this wouldn't happen again? Then why had it?

Because you wanted it, an inner voice said. *You wanted it and you got it.*

She leaned back and their gazes locked. Before she could say anything, he lowered his mouth to hers. The kiss was slow, languid, penetrating and as hot as any kiss could be. His tongue wrapped around hers...or had hers wrapped around his?

Did it matter?

Not when he was using that tongue to massage every inch of her mouth from top to bottom, front to back. The juncture of her legs began to throb again as if they hadn't been satisfied just moments ago.

She broke off the kiss to look into eyes that were dark with desire once again. And she knew this was just the beginning.

Later, Adrian would question how Trinity had managed, quite nicely and relatively thoroughly, to get into his system. He would also question why, after making love to her at least two more times in the bedroom, he was still wanting her in a way he had never wanted another woman.

"Tell me your other reason," she asked, breaking into his thoughts.

She was spread on top of him. Her hair was all over her head, in her face. Her mouth looked as though it had been kissed way too many times. Her eyes were still glazed from a recent orgasm or two, possibly three. She looked simply beautiful.

"My other reason?" he asked, his brow rising.

"Yes, your other reason for dropping by here tonight. You said there were two."

So he had. "Tomorrow night. Do you have any plans?"

She seemed to think about his question for a quick second. "Granted I get to leave the hospital on time without Belvedere finding a reason to make me work late…no, I don't have any plans. Why?"

"I want to invite you to dinner. In Westmoreland Country."

She nervously licked her lips. "Dinner with your family?"

"Yes."

She didn't say anything for a minute. "They know about us?" she asked. "About this?"

He shook his head. "Depends on what part you're referring to. They know I've been your pretend lover, but as far as the transition to the real thing, no."

She pulled back slightly. "What would they think if they found out the truth?"

He chuckled. "Other than thinking Thorn is going to kick my ass, probably nothing."

"Why would Thorn do that?"

"He thinks of you as a kid sister."

She shook her head. "He used to. Now he thinks of me as an adult. I guess he's mellowed over the years."

He wondered if they were talking about the same Thorn Westmoreland. "If you say so. So what about it? Will you go with me to the chow-down tomorrow night?"

"Yes."

For some reason her answer made his night. "I'll pick you up around six, okay?"

"All right. I'll be ready."

Adrian gathered her close to him, thinking, *So will I.*

Fifteen

As Trinity moved through the hospital corridors checking on her patients, she couldn't help but notice she felt well-rested, although for two nights straight she'd participated in a sexual marathon. That she had left Adrian in her bed after a romp of the best morning sex ever was something she tried not to think about, but when she did she couldn't help but smile.

He'd told her he'd wanted to make sure she left for work with a smile on her face and that was one mission he'd accomplished. She was in a cheerful mood this morning and was determined not to let anything or anyone ruin her day, including Dr. Belvedere.

She had seen him when she'd first arrived but he'd been rushing off to the operating room. According to one of the nurses, he was scheduled for surgery most of the day. That only added to her cheerfulness. The less she saw of the man, the better.

She pulled her phone out of her jacket when she heard a text come through. She smiled even wider after reading the message.

Think of me today.

She smiled and texted back.

Only if you think of me.

Adrian's reply was quick.

Done.

She chuckled to herself and put her phone back in her jacket.

"I see something has you in a good mood, Dr. Matthews."

Her body automatically cringed at the sound of Casey Belvedere's voice. He moved to stand in front of her, still wearing his surgical attire. Why wasn't he still in surgery? "Yes, Dr. Belvedere, I am in a good mood."

"And you look well rested," he noted.

"I am." *No thanks to you,* she thought but said, "The nurses said you had several surgeries this morning."

"I do, but the one I just completed was finished ahead of schedule so I have a little time to spare. Share a cup of coffee with me?"

"No, thank you. I need to check on my patients."

"Not if I say you shouldn't."

She lifted her chin and fought a glare. "Surely you're not asking me to put my patients' needs on hold just for me to share a cup of coffee with you, Dr. Belvedere?"

He frowned and took a step closer under the pretense of looking at the chart she was holding. "Don't ever chastise me again, Dr. Matthews. Don't forget who I am. All it would take is one word from me and I can ruin your career before it gets started. And as far as that boyfriend of yours, I meant what I said. Get rid of him. You'll be doing yourself a favor.

"I had him checked out. He's one of *those* Westmorelands. Although he and his family might have a little money, I recall that he, his siblings and his cousin were known troublemakers when they were younger. Nothing but little delinquents. My parents sent me to private schools all my life just so I wouldn't have to deal with people like them. I come from old money, his family comes from—"

"Money that's obtained from hard work and sacrifices," she said curtly, refusing to let him put down Adrian or his family.

Belvedere opened his mouth to say something just as his name blasted from the speaker requesting that he return to the surgical wing. He glared at her. "We'll finish this conversation later." Turning quickly, he was gone.

Trinity felt shaken to the core. The look on Belvedere's face had sent chills up her spine. The man definitely had a problem. If her pretend-lover plan wasn't working and if the hospital administrators and the chief of pediatrics also refused to acknowledge his continued harassment of her, then there was nothing left for her to do but to put in a request to be transferred to another hospital, one as far away from Denver as she could get. She would start the paperwork later today.

"So what do you think?"

After having read Stern's assessment report on the Texas project slated to start in the fall, Adrian smiled. "I think you outlined all the legal ramifications nicely. We were lucky to get top bid on that property, especially since Dallas is booming."

"Yes it is," Stern agreed, dropping down into the chair in front of Adrian's desk. "So, are you joining the family tonight for the chow-down?"

"Yes, and I'm bringing Trinity with me."

Stern nodded. "How are things going with the two of you pretending to be having an affair? Has that doctor backed off yet?"

"No." Adrian spent the next ten minutes telling Stern about Belvedere's treatment of Trinity.

"I can't believe the bastard," Stern railed angrily. "Who the hell does he think he is? He better be glad he's dealing with Trinity and not JoJo. She would have kicked his ass all over the hospital by now."

Adrian fought back a smile knowing that was true. Stern's fiancée, Jovonnie Jones, was not only an ace in martial arts but she could handle a bow and arrow and firearms pretty damn nicely, as well.

"Trinity has to be careful how she handles the situation, man. The Belvedere name carries a lot of weight in this city and the administrators at the hospital refuse to do anything to stop him."

"Why wait for them? I wouldn't even be having this conversation with the old Adrian. He would have whipped somebody's behind by now. He would not allow anyone to mess with his girlfriend."

"Trinity is not my girlfriend."

"But the doctor doesn't know that and he's given you no respect. Who the hell does he think he is to hit on another man's woman? Man, you've mellowed too much over the years."

"Just trying to keep the family's name clean, Stern. You should understand that, considering my history. Besides, Dillon gave me a warning not to take matters into my own hands."

Stern leaned closer to the desk. "As far as I'm concerned, in this case, what Dillon doesn't know won't hurt him."

"I agree," a deep voice said from across the room. "So when can we go kick the doctor's ass?"

Stern and Adrian turned. Towering in the doorway, and looking more physically fit than any man had a right to look, was Bane Westmoreland.

"And you're sure that's what you want to do, Trinity?"

Trinity could hear the concern in her sister's voice and she knew she had to assure Tara she was okay with her decision. "Of course it's not what I want to do, Tara. If I had my way I would finish up my residency in Denver but that's not possible. Putting in for a transfer is for the best."

"You and Adrian pretending to be lovers didn't help, I guess?"

"No. Belvedere expects me to break up with Adrian. He's just that conceited to think I will drop someone for him."

"There has to be another way."

"I wish there was but there's not. I could go beyond the hospital administrators to the commissioner of hospitals for the State of Colorado, but then it would be Belvedere's word against mine. The case might drag out for no telling how long. Or worse yet, he might try to turn the tables and claim I'm the one who came on to him. It will take time and money to prove my case, and I don't have either. All I want to do is complete my residency, not waste time facing Casey Belvedere in court. Besides, if I pursue this, his family might stop the funding for a children's wing that's badly needed at Denver Memorial."

When her sister didn't say anything, Trinity added, "Hey, it won't be so bad. You transferred to another hospital during your residency and did fine. In fact, by doing so you were able to connect with Thorn."

"Yes, but I left Kentucky because I wanted to leave, not because I felt I had to."

"I appreciate all you tried to do," Trinity said after a pause. "Coming up with the idea for me and Adrian to pretend to be lovers was wonderful. Any other man would have backed off. But not Belvedere. The word *entitled* is written all over him. He assumes he has the right to have me, boyfriend or no boyfriend—how crazy is that?"

She glanced at her watch. "I need to get dressed. Adrian invited me to the Westmorelands' for dinner tonight. It's their weekly Friday night chow-down."

"That was nice of him."

"Yes, it was," Trinity agreed.

"Are you going to tell Adrian about the transfer?"

"Nothing to tell yet. I just put in for it today and it will probably take a few weeks before a hospital picks me up. I'll mention it when I know where I'll be going. He's been so nice about everything." She wouldn't tell Tara how their relationship was no longer a pretense because she knew even that was short term.

"Well, the two of you won't have to pretend to be lovers anymore now."

No, they wouldn't, Trinity thought. Why did that realization bother her? Trinity pulled herself up from the sofa. "Okay, Tara, I need to get dressed."

"Tell everyone I said hello and I look forward to seeing them at Stern's wedding in June."

"I will." Trinity knew if things worked out the way she wanted with the transfer, by June she would have left Denver and would hopefully be working at some hospital on the east coast.

After clicking off the phone with Tara, Trinity headed for the bedroom. She refused to question why she was anxious to see Adrian again.

"When did you get home?"

"Does Dillon know you're here?"

"What's been going on with you?"

"We haven't heard from you in over a year."

Bane Westmoreland grinned at all the questions being thrown at him. "I came straight here from the airport and, no, Dil doesn't know I'm here. I've been busy and you haven't heard from me because of assignments I can't talk about. All I can say is it's good to be home, although I'll only be here for a few days."

Adrian studied his cousin and noted how much Bane had changed over the years. When Bane had left home to join the navy he had been angry, heartbroken and disillusioned. Personally, Adrian had given the navy less than six months before they tossed out the badass Bane. But Bane had proved Adrian wrong by hanging in and making the most of it. Now Bane stood taller, walked straighter and smiled more often. Although there was no doubt in Adrian's mind his cousin was still a badass.

"So where's Dillon? All his secretary would say is that he's away from the office," Bane said.

"He had a meeting with several potential clients and won't be back until later this evening. He's going to be surprised as hell to see you," Adrian said, grinning. He couldn't wait to see Dillon's face when Dillon saw his baby brother. Of all the younger Westmorelands that Dillon had become responsible for, Bane had been the biggest challenge. Dillon was the one who had finally talked Bane into moving away, joining the military to get his life together... and leaving Crystal Newsome alone.

Crystal Newsome...

Adrian wondered if Bane knew where Crystal was or if he even cared after all this time. All the family knew was that the two obsessed-with-each-other teens had needed to be separated. Crystal's parents had sent her to live with an aunt somewhere and Dillon had convinced Bane to go into the military.

"You returned home at the perfect time, Bane," Stern

noted. "Tonight is the chow-down and we're celebrating JoJo's birthday."

Bane smiled. "That's great. How is she doing? I heard about her father's death a while back. She's still your best friend, right?"

It occurred to Adrian that because Bane had been on assignments and hadn't been home since Megan and Rico's wedding, he didn't know about any of the family's recent news—like the babies, other family weddings and the engagements.

Bane had a lot of catching up to do and Adrian couldn't wait to bring his cousin up to date.

Sixteen

Trinity watched herself in the mirror as she slid lipstick across her lips. Why had she gone to such great pains to make sure she looked good tonight when all she was doing was joining Adrian and his family for dinner? No big deal. So why was she making it one?

One second passed and then another while she stood staring at her reflection, thinking of the possible answers for that particular question. When her heart rate picked up, she frowned at the image staring back at her.

"No, we aren't going there. I am *not* developing feelings for Adrian. I am *not!* It's all about getting the best sex I ever had. Any woman would become infatuated with a man who could give them multiple orgasms all through the night, without breaking a sweat."

And she didn't want to think about the times he had sweated. *Lordy!* Those times were too hot to think about.

She turned when she heard her cell phone ring and disappointment settled in her stomach. That special ring meant it was the hospital calling because she was needed due to an emergency. That also meant she would have to cancel her dinner date with Adrian.

She clicked on her phone. "This is Dr. Matthews."

"Dr. Matthews, this is Dr. Belvedere."

Trinity stiffened at the sound of the man's voice and tried to maintain control of her anger. Why was he calling her? Typically, whenever there was an emergency, the call would come from one of the hospital's administrative assistants, never from any of the doctors. Most were too busy taking care of patients.

"Yes, Dr. Belvedere?"

"Just wanted you to know I'll be leaving town for two weeks. They need medical volunteers to help out where that tornado touched down in Texas. They want the best so of course that includes me."

She rolled her eyes. "Is there a reason you're informing me of this?"

"Yes, because when I get back I expect things to change. I'm tired of playing these silly games with you."

Silly games with her? Her body tensed. "You're tired of playing games with me? I think you have that backward, Dr. Belvedere. I'm the one who is tired of your games. I told you I have no interest in a relationship with you. I don't understand why you can't accept that as final."

"Nothing is final until I say so. I would suggest you remember that. When I get back I want changes in your attitude or you'll be kicked out of the residency program."

She wanted to scream that he didn't have to waste his time kicking her out because she was leaving on her own, but she bit back the words. She would let him find that out on his own. Hopefully it would be after the approval for a transfer came in.

"Do whatever you think you need to do because I will never go out with you. Goodbye, Dr. Belvedere."

"We'll see about that. You've got two weeks."

Refusing to engage in conversation with him any longer, she clicked off the phone, closed her eyes and sucked in a deep breath. He had ruined what had started off as a cheerful day, and she simply refused to allow the man to ruin her evening, as well.

Adrian pulled into Trinity's driveway feeling pretty good about today. Bane's arrival had been a surprise for everyone and catching him up on family matters had been priceless. Bane was shocked as hell to find out about all the marriages that had taken place—Zane's especially. And for Bane to discover he was an uncle to Canyon's son Beau was worth leaving the office and sharing drinks to celebrate at McKays.

That was another thing that had been priceless. News that Bane had returned home for a visit traveled fast, and when he walked into McKays it was obvious some of the patrons were ready to run for cover. Bane's reputation in Denver preceded him and it hadn't been good. But some were willing to let bygones be bygones, especially those who'd heard Bane had attended the naval academy—graduating nearly top of his class—and was now a navy SEAL. They took the time to congratulate him on his accomplishments. Everyone knew it had taken hard work, dedication and discipline—things the old Bane had lacked. The badass native son had returned and everyone told him how proud they were of him.

Then there was Bane's reunion with Bailey. Canyon had called to tell her Bane was in town and she'd met them at the restaurant. She was there waiting and one might have thought she and Bane hadn't seen each other in years. Seeing them together, hugging tight, made Adrian realize just how the four of them—him, Aidan, Bane and Bailey—had bonded during those turbulent years after losing their parents. They'd thought that getting into trouble was the only way to expel their grief.

Getting out of his car now, Adrian headed toward Trinity's front door. He couldn't wait to get her to Westmoreland Country and introduce her to Bane. His cousin had heard enough of Adrian's conversation with Stern to know what was going on with Trinity and Dr. Belvedere. Bane agreed with Stern that Adrian should work the doctor over. Specifically, break a couple of his precious fingers. Adrian was still trying to follow Dillon's advice.

Trinity opened the door within seconds of his first knock and all he could say was *wow*. Adrian wasn't sure what about her tonight made him do a double take. He figured he could blame it on her short sweater dress, leggings and boots, all of which put some mighty fine curves on display. Or it could be the way she'd styled her hair—falling loosely to her shoulders.

But really he knew that what had desire thrumming through him was nothing more than Trinity simply being Trinity.

"Aren't you going to say anything?"

He forced his attention away from her luscious mouth to gaze into a pair of adorable brown eyes. He took her hand, entered her home and closed the door behind him. "I'm known as a man of few words, but a lot of action," he said in a husky voice as a smile curved the corners of his mouth.

He tugged her closer while placing his hand at the small of her back. They were chest to chest and he noted her heartbeats were coming in just as fast and strong as his. His gaze latched on to the lips he'd been mesmerized by just moments ago. Their shape had a way of making him hard anytime he concentrated on them for too long. And tonight they were glazed with a beguiling shade of fuchsia.

He leaned in and licked the seam of her lips. Her heart rate increased with every stroke of his tongue. When her lips parted on a breathless sigh, he took the opportunity to seize, conquer and devour. He hadn't realized just how hungry he was for her taste. How could kissing any woman bring him to this? Wanting her so badly that needing to make love to her was like a tangible force.

She suddenly pulled back, breaking off the kiss. She touched her lips. "I think they're swollen."

He smiled. "Better there than there," he said, moving his gaze to an area below her waist. His eyes moved back up to her face and he saw the deep coloring in her cheeks. Honestly? She could blush after everything he'd done to her between those gorgeous legs?

"Your family is going to know."

He quirked a brow. "What? That I kissed you?"

"Yes."

She was right—his family would know. They had a tendency to notice just about everything. But Bane's surprise visit might preoccupy them. However, his family was his family and preoccupied or not, they had the propensity to pick up on stuff. So, if she thought they could keep what was really going on between them a secret, then she wasn't thinking straight. He decided to let her find that out for herself.

He took her hand. "Ready?"

"I need to repair my lipstick."

"All right."

He watched her walk off toward her bedroom and decided not to tell her that before the night was over, she would be repairing it several more times.

A few hours later Trinity was remembering just how much fun being around a family could be. The Westmorelands, she'd discovered whenever she visited Tara in Atlanta, were a fun-loving group who enjoyed spending time together. And it seemed the Denver clan was no different.

It appeared tonight was especially festive with the return of the infamous Brisbane Westmoreland, whom everyone called Bane. Although he'd mentioned he would be home for only three days before embarking on another assignment, his family already had a slew of activities for him to engage in while he was here.

Bane mentioned he would not be attending Stern's wedding in June, saying he would be out of the country for a while. Trinity figured he would be on some secret mission. He looked the part of a navy SEAL with his height and his muscular build, and he was definitely a handsome man. His eyes were a beautiful shade of hazel that blended well with his mocha complexion. As far as she'd seen, no other Westmoreland had eyes that color. When she asked Adrian about it, he'd said their great-grandmother Gemma had hazel eyes, and so far Bane was the only other Westmoreland who'd inherited that eye color.

Everyone was sitting at the table enjoying the delicious dinner the Westmoreland ladies had prepared. It amazed her how well the women in this family got along. They acted more like sisters than sisters-in-law. Pam had told Trinity that hosting a chow-down every Friday night was a way for the family to stay connected. Earlier, they had gathered in the living room to sing happy birthday to Stern's fiancée, JoJo.

Adrian sat beside Trinity and more than once he leaned over to ask if she was enjoying herself. And she would readily assure him that she was.

"I hope you don't mind, Trinity, but Dillon mentioned the trouble you're having with some doctor at the hospital," Rico Claiborne, who was married to Adrian's sister Megan, said.

She looked down the table to where Rico sat beside Megan and across from Bane. "Yes. Adrian and I thought claiming to be in an exclusive relationship would make him back off, but it didn't. He even had the gall to tell me to end my relationship with Adrian or else." She could tell by the expressions on everyone's faces that they were shocked at Belvedere's audacity.

"Have you thought about recording any of the conversations he's having with you?" Rico asked. "Evidently the man feels he can say and do whatever suits him. There is such a thing as sexual harassment no matter how many hospital wings his family builds."

Trinity nodded. "No, I hadn't thought about it. I assumed taping someone's conversation without their knowledge was illegal."

"That's true in some states but not here in Colorado," Keisha, Canyon's wife, who was an attorney, advised. "Only thing is, if he suspects the conversation is being recorded and asks if it is, you're legally obligated to tell him yes. Otherwise it's not admissible in a court of law," she added.

"Recording his conversations might be something you want to consider, Trinity," Adrian said thoughtfully.

She nodded. It was definitely something she would consider. Although her plan now was to leave Denver and transfer to another hospital, what Rico suggested might be useful if Belvedere tried to block the transfer or give her a hard time about it. At this point she wouldn't put anything past him.

"That might be a good idea," she conceded. "At least I'll have him out of my hair for two weeks." She then told everyone about the phone call she had received earlier from Casey Belvedere and the things he had said. By the time she finished she could tell everyone seated at the table was upset about it.

"Why didn't you tell me about that call when I came to pick you up?" Adrian asked.

She could tell he could barely control his anger. "I didn't want to ruin our evening, but it looks like I did anyway.

Sorry, everyone, I shouldn't be dumping my problems on you."

"No need to apologize," Dillon said, seated at the head of the long table. "The plan that Tara came up with for you and Adrian to pretend to be in an exclusive relationship didn't work, so now you should go to plan B. I agree with Rico that getting those harassing conversations recorded will help."

"I can almost guarantee they will," Rico said, leaning back in his chair. "And I've got the perfect item you can wear without anyone, including the doctor, knowing his words are being recorded. It resembles a woman's necklace and all you have to do is touch it to begin taping. Piece of cake. Let's meet right before the doctor gets back in town and set things up."

Trinity smiled. "Okay. That sounds like a great plan."

"I had such a great time tonight, Adrian. Your family is super. Thanks for inviting me."

Adrian followed her through the door, closing it behind them. He had gotten angry when Trinity had told everyone what Belvedere had said to her, and he hadn't been able to get his anger back in check since. The man had a lot of damn nerve.

"Adrian?"

Upon hearing his name he glanced across the room. Trinity had already removed her jacket, taken off her boots and was plopping down on her sofa.

"Yes?"

"I was telling you how much I enjoyed myself tonight, but you weren't listening. You okay?"

"Yes, I'm fine," he lied, moving to join her on the sofa. Truth of the matter was, he wasn't okay. A part of him was still seething. He had a mind to forget about what Dillon had said and go over to Belvedere's place and do as

Bane had suggested and give him a good kick in the ass. How dare that man continue to try to make a move on his woman and…

It suddenly hit him solidly in the gut that Trinity wasn't *his woman*. However, for the past couple of nights she'd been his bed partner. He cringed at the sound of that. He'd had bed partners before, plenty of them, so why did classifying her in that category bother him?

She twisted around on the sofa to face him, tucking her legs beneath her. "No, I don't think you're fine. There's something bothering you, I can tell. You were even quiet on the drive back here, so tell me what's going on."

It was on the tip of his tongue to reassure her again that he was okay but he knew she wouldn't believe him. He decided to be honest. "Belvedere's phone call has me angry." He shook his head. "He has a lot of damn gall. And what's so sad is that he doesn't see anything wrong with his behavior, mainly because no one has yet to call him out on it. He feels he can get away with it. You should have told me about that call earlier, Trinity."

She frowned. "Why? It would only have ruined our evening. I regret mentioning it at all. The man was behaving as his usual asinine self."

Adrian stared at her, finally realizing the full impact of the crap she'd been going through for the past six months. This hadn't been just a few words exchanged now and then, but bull she'd had to put up with constantly.

He cupped her face in his hands. "Neither you nor any woman should have to put up with that. I don't just want Belvedere gone, but I want the top administrator of the hospital gone as well. The moment you went to him and complained, something should have been done."

"I agree, but that's politics, Adrian, not just at Denver Memorial but at a number of hospitals. That's how the game is played. Some people with money assume their wealth comes with power. The Belvederes evidently fall within that category. They are big philanthropists who support great causes. Only thing is, their gift comes with a price. Maybe not to the hospital who's grateful to get that new wing, but to innocent people…in this case women who are—doctors, nurses, aids. Women they can prey on sexually. Yes, there are laws against that sort of thing, but first the law has to be enforced."

She paused and then added, "I doubt it would have made any difference to Belvedere if I was married. A husband would not stand in the way of getting whatever he wanted. And I bet I'm not an isolated case. There were probably others before me. He's trying to hold my career hostage to get his way. Some other woman might feel forced to eventually give in to him. But not me. However, I know fighting him is useless, which is why I've completed paperwork for a transfer to another hospital."

Thunderstruck, Adrian's blood pounded fast and furious at his temples. "Transfer? You've applied for a transfer?"

"Yes."

His muscles tensed. "To another hospital here in Denver?"

"No. I don't know of any hospital in this city that the Belvedere name is not associated with somehow. I'm hoping to relocate to the east coast, closer to home."

He was quiet as he absorbed what she'd said. In a way he shouldn't be surprised. She'd told him more than once that she didn't like big cities and Denver hadn't really impressed her. All she'd been doing since moving here was putting up with crap. Still…

"When were you going to tell me about the transfer?" he asked. The thought that she had put in for one and hadn't mentioned it bothered him.

"I planned to tell you once I got word it went through.

There was no reason to tell you beforehand. I just put in the paperwork today."

No reason to tell him. Of course she would feel that way since all you are is a bed partner, man.

"But why today? Did something else happen that you haven't mentioned?" When she had left for work this morning she'd been in a good mood. He'd made certain of it.

She shrugged. "Nothing other than Belvedere being his usual narcissistic self. But he did something today that really got to me."

"What?"

She hesitated, as if trying to control her emotions. "I had patients to see, yet he wanted me to forget about their needs to go somewhere and have a cup of coffee with him. How selfish can one man be? I couldn't stand him as a man but after that conversation I no longer respected him as a doctor. It was then that I decided not to put up with it any longer."

"Just like that?"

"Yes, just like that."

He could appreciate her decision since no one—man or woman—should have to put up with a hostile work environment, especially when that environment was supposed to be about the business of caring for people.

"So, if you plan on leaving the hospital anyway, why did you lead Rico to believe you want to record one of those harassing conversations with Belvedere?"

"Because I do. The paperwork for the transfer will probably take a while to get approved. Once he finds out about it he might try blocking it or give me a low approval rating where no other hospital will take me. I can't let that happen. I need leverage and I will get it."

He heard the determination in her voice. She had worked hard for her medical degree. He of all people knew how hard that was since his twin, Aidan, had gone through the process. No person should have the right to tear down what it took another person more than eight years to build.

Adrian agreed that she needed peace of mind in her work, so she didn't have to worry about some crazy jerk trying to force her into his bed. The thought of her leaving Denver and moving on should have no bearing on him or his life whatsoever, but somehow it did.

At the moment, he didn't want to try to figure it out. All he knew was that she didn't need him anymore.

"Since you're moving to plan B, I guess that pretty much concludes plan A," he said, standing. He had been plan A.

She looked up at him, confused. "What do you mean?"

"You're going to expose Belvedere with that recording, so we don't have to pretend to be lovers anymore."

He watched her expression and knew the thought hadn't crossed her mind. She stood, sliding off the sofa in a fluid movement any man would appreciate. She wrapped her arms around his waist. "We stopped *pretending* to be lovers that night at your house, Adrian."

He felt the way her heart was beating, fast and powerful, a mirror of his own. And he saw the look in her eyes, glazed with desire. "Define our relationship, Trinity." He wanted her to establish her expectations.

She nervously licked her lips and his gaze followed the movement. A spike of heat hit him in the gut, making his erection throb. He wanted her and was, as usual, amazed at the intensity of his desire for her.

"It will be an affair with no promises or expectations, Adrian. I'm leaving Denver as soon as the transfer comes through and I won't look back. We're good together. You make me feel things I've never felt before. I want to get it all while I can. I figure the next few years of my life will involve working harder than ever to rebuild the momentum I've lost here. An involvement with anyone won't happen for a long time."

A fleeting smile touched her lips. "That means I need you to help me stock up on all the sex I can get. Think you can handle that?"

Oh, he could handle it, but...

Why did accepting her terms feel so difficult for him? Hadn't he presented the same terms—no promises or expectations—to a number of women? He didn't like being tied down, he liked dating, and he enjoyed the freedom of having to answer to no woman. And he definitely enjoyed sex. So why did her definition of what they would be sharing bother him? He should be overjoyed that she was a woman who thought the way he did.

He looked down at her, and knew he would accept whatever way she wanted things to be. "Yes, I can handle it."

"I knew you could."

She lowered her hands from his waist and cupped him through his pants. He didn't have to ask what she was doing because he knew. She was going after what she wanted, and he had no intention of stopping her.

She undressed him, intermittently placing kisses all over his body as each piece of clothing was removed. And then he undressed her.

"Make me scream, Adrian," she whispered when she stood in front of him totally naked.

"Baby, I intend to. All over the place."

He swept her into his arms and headed toward her bedroom.

Seventeen

"I am definitely going to miss this," Trinity said, collapsing on the broad expanse of Adrian's chest. The memory of a back-to-back orgasm was still vivid in her mind, its impact still strong on her body.

"Then don't go."

She somehow found the strength to raise her head and gaze into a pair of dark brown eyes. Although he had a serious look on his face, she knew he was joking. He had put his social life on hold while pretending to be her lover, and she knew the minute she left Denver it would be business as usual for him.

"You're just saying that because you know I intend to wear you out over the next few weeks," she said, leaning up to lick the underside of his jaw.

She watched him smile before he said, "I'd like to see you try."

Inwardly, she knew there was no way she could try and live to boast about it. The man had more stamina than a raging bull. He definitely knew how to make her scream.

Scream...

She had done that aplenty. It was a wonder her neighbors hadn't called the police. He shifted positions to cuddle her by tightening his arms around her and throwing his leg over hers. It was such an intimate position being spooned next to him. There was nothing like having his still engorged penis pressed against her backside.

She looked over her shoulder at him. "Tell me about your childhood with your cousins. I heard that you, Aidan, Bane and Bailey were a handful." She wouldn't mention that Dr. Belvedere had referred to them as little delinquents.

Adrian didn't say anything for the longest moment, and she began to wonder if he would answer when he told her in a low tone, "You don't know how often over the past eight to ten years that the four of us have probably apologized to Dillon, Ramsey...the entire family for our behavior during the time we lost our parents. That had to be the hardest thing we had to go through. One day they were here and the next day they were gone, and knowing we wouldn't see them again was too much for us.

"But Dillon and the others were there, trying to do what they could to make the pain easier to bear, but the pain went too deep. The state tried forcing Dillon to put us in the system, but he refused, and had to actually fight them in court."

He paused again. "That's one of the main reasons I work so hard now to make them proud of me, to show the family that their investment in my future, their undying love and commitment, didn't go to waste."

She heard the deep emotion in his voice and flipped onto her back to stare up at him. "Were the four of you *that* bad?"

"Probably worse than you can even imagine. We didn't do drugs or anything like that, just did a lot of mischievous deeds that got us into trouble with the law."

"Gangs?" she asked curiously.

He chuckled. "The four of us were our own gang and would take on anyone who messed with us. I truly don't know how Dillon dealt with us. Convincing Bane to leave home for the military was the best thing he could have done. And Bailey finally got tired of getting her mouth washed out with soap because of her filthy language."

"Dillon must be proud of the men and woman the four of you have become."

Adrian smiled. "He says he is, although he considers us works-in-progress. We're older, more mature and a lot smarter than way back then. But he probably can't help but get nervous whenever the four of us get together."

"Dillon seemed relaxed tonight."

"He was to a degree, probably because Aidan was missing. I figure it will be a while before he completely lets his guard down where the four of us are concerned."

"But I'm sure that day will come," she said with certainty. "Now I want to know about your college days. Did you have a lot of girlfriends?"

He chuckled. "Of course. But they could never be certain if it was really me or Aidan they were dating. We're identical and there's only one way to tell us apart."

She lifted a brow. "And which way is that?"

He eyed her as if trying to decide if she could be trusted with such valuable information. "Our hands."

"Your hands?"

"Yes." He held up his right hand. "I have this tiny scar here," he said, indicating the small mark right beneath his thumb. "I got this when I was a kid, trying to climb a tree. Before that, no one could tell us apart. Not even Dillon and Ramsey."

"So you played a lot of tricks on people."

"You know it. Basically all the time. Even freaked out our teachers. We liked dong that. I think the only people who could tell us apart without checking our hands were Bane and Bailey."

Then they talked about her childhood. She practically had him rolling in laughter when she told him how she'd tried to get rid of one of her brother's girlfriends that she didn't like. And she told him of the one and only time she'd gotten into trouble in school.

"You were a relatively good girl," he said.

"Still am. Don't you think I'm *good?*"

He grinned. "No argument out of me."

She returned his grin. "You're a softy."

"No," he said as his gaze suddenly darkened. "I'm hard. Feel me."

She did. Now his erection was poking her in the thigh. If anyone would have told her she would find herself in this position with a man a few months ago, she would not have believed them.

"You leave for work early in the morning—are you ready to go to sleep?"

"I should be ready, shouldn't I?"

"Yes."

She had shared his bed for three days straight now and she couldn't help wondering how things would be when she left Denver and he was no longer there to keep her warm at night. What would happen when those tingling sensations came and he wasn't there to satisfy them?

She felt his already hard penis thicken against her thigh. He'd practically answered the question for her. No, she wasn't ready to go to sleep and it seemed neither was he.

"Have I ever told you how much I love touching you?" he asked, running a hand over her breasts, caressing the tips of her nipples. The action caused a stirring in the pit of her stomach.

"I don't think that you have."

"Then I'm falling down on the job," he said, moving his hand away from her breasts to travel to the area between her thighs. She knew he would find her wet and ready.

"And speaking of *down.*" He shifted his body to place his head between her thighs. After spreading her legs and lifting her hips, his tongue began making love to her in slow, deep strokes.

He held tight to her hips, refusing to let them go. She groaned and as if he'd been waiting to hear that sound, he began flicking his tongue. She grabbed hold of his head to hold him there. *Yes, right there.*

She closed her eyes, taking in the sound of him, the feel of him. This had to be one of the most erotic things a man could do to a woman. And she was convinced no one could do it better than Adrian.

Her body was poised to go off the deep end, when suddenly Adrian released her hips, flipped her around, tilted her hips and entered her in one smooth thrust.

"I like doing it this way," he whispered, taking her in long, powerful strokes as he placed butterfly kisses along the back of her neck.

She liked doing it this way, too. Trinity cried out as spasms consumed her body. He kept going and going and she was the recipient of the most stimulating strokes known to womankind.

When he let out a deep, guttural growl, she felt him, the full essence of him, shoot into her. That's when she lost it and let out a deep, soul-wrenching scream of ecstasy.

Eventually he gathered her into his arms and pulled her to him. Their breathing labored, he cuddled her close to his chest. The last thing she remembered was the deep, husky sound of his voice whispering, "Now you can go to sleep, baby."

And she did.

Several days later, Adrian scanned the room, seeing eager expressions on the faces of his family members. Rico had called this meeting to give them an update. For the past year Rico's PI firm had been investigating the connection of four women—Portia, Lila, Clarice and Isabelle—to their great-grandfather, Raphel Westmoreland.

For the longest time the family had assumed their great-grandmother Gemma was their great-grandfather's only wife. However, it had been discovered during a genealogy search that before marrying Gemma, Raphel had been connected to four other women who'd been listed as his wives.

The mystery of Portia and Lila had been solved. They hadn't been wives but women Raphel had helped out of sticky situations. It was, however, discovered that the woman named Clarice had given birth to a son that Raphel had never known about. Upon Clarice's death in a train accident, that son was adopted by a woman by the name of Jeanette Outlaw. Rico's firm was still trying to locate any living relatives of the child Jeanette had adopted. The news Rico had just delivered was about the woman named Isabelle.

"So you're saying Raphel's only connection to Isabelle was that he came across her homeless and penniless? After she had a child out of wedlock and her parents kicked her out? He gave her a place to live?" Dillon asked.

"Yes. The child was not Raphel's. He allowed her to live at his place since he was not home most of the time while riding the herds. As soon as she got on her feet, she moved out. Eventually, Isabelle met someone. An older gentleman, a widower by the name of Hogan Nelson who had three children of his own. Isabelle and Hogan eventually married. Your grandfather Raphel was introduced to your grandmother Gemma by Isabelle. Gemma was Hogan and Isabelle's babysitter."

Megan nodded. "So that's why Gemma and Isabelle were from the same town of Percy, Nevada."

"Yes," Rico said, smiling at his wife. "It seems your great-grandfather had a reputation for coming to the aid of women in distress. A regular good guy. Of the four women, the only one he was romantically involved with was Clarice."

"Have you been able to find out anything about the family of Raphel and Clarice's son, Levy Outlaw?" Pam asked.

Rico shook his head. "Not yet. That's an ongoing investigation. We traced the man and his family to Detroit but haven't been able to pick up the trail from there."

A few moments later the meeting ended. Adrian was about to leave when Dillon stopped him.

"You okay?"

He smiled at his cousin. "Yes, Dil, I'm fine."

He nodded. "I talked to Thorn last night and he told me about Trinity putting in for a transfer. How do you feel about that?"

Adrian decided to be honest about it. "Not good. I knew she would eventually leave Denver, but she is being forced to leave and I don't like it one damn bit. Denver Memorial has not treated her fairly."

Dillon nodded. "No, they haven't."

Adrian ran a frustrated hand down his face. "I can't help wondering what happens when Trinity leaves. Who will Belvedere target next? He has to be stopped."

Trinity wished the days weren't passing so quickly. Two weeks were almost up and in a few days Casey Belvedere would be returning. She had hoped her transfer would have come through by now but it hadn't.

She had met with Rico and he had given her the necklace and had showed her how it worked. He'd stressed the importance of setting it to record the minute Belvedere began talking. He also said she shouldn't deliberately lead the doctor into any particular conversation. She didn't want to make it seem as if she was deliberately trapping him. It had to be obvious that he was the one initiating the unwanted conversations.

She stopped folding laundry when she received a text on her phone. She smiled when she saw it was from Adrian.

Want to go out to dinner? Millennium Place?

She texted him back.

Dinner at MP sounds nice.

Great. Pick you up around 7.

Trinity slid her phone back into the pocket of her jeans. Adrian had taken her at her word about wanting to be with him as much as possible. Every night they either slept at her place or she spent the night at his.

The more time she spent with him the more she discovered about him and the more she liked him. He hated broccoli and loved strawberry ice cream. Brown was his favorite color. In addition to mountain climbing, he enjoyed skiing and often joined his cousin Riley on the slopes each year.

Trinity glanced at her watch. Adrian said he would pick her up at seven, which would only give her an hour to get ready. Millennium Place was one of those swanky restaurants that usually required reservations well in advance. Evidently, Adrian had a connection, which didn't surprise her.

At seven o'clock Adrian rang her doorbell and after giving her outfit and makeup one last check in the full-length mirror, she answered the door, trying to ignore the tingling sensations in her stomach.

The sight of him almost took her breath away. He looked dashing in his dark suit. He handed her a red, long-stemmed rose. "Hi, beautiful. This is for you."

She accepted the gift as he came inside. "What's this for?"

"Just because," he said, smiling. "You look gorgeous."

"Thanks and thank you for the rose. And I happen to think you look gorgeous, as well."

He chuckled. "Ready to go? Dinner is awaiting this gorgeous couple."

Smiling, she said, "Yes, I'm ready."

She bit back the temptation to say *"for you always,"* and wondered why she would even think such a thing. She knew it wasn't possible.

Eighteen

Adrian held up his glass of champagne. "I propose a toast."

Trinity smiled and held up hers, as well. "To what?"

"Not to what but to whom. You."

She chuckled. "To me?"

"Yes, to you *and* to me. It was a month ago tonight we went out on our first date. Regardless of the reason, you must admit it ended pretty nicely. You have to admit it's been fun."

"Yes," she said. "It's been fun."

Their glasses clinked. As Adrian took a sip of the bubbly he recalled his conversation with Dillon. On the drive over to pick up Trinity he'd kept imagining how his life would be once she left town.

He placed his glass down and studied her. He'd made a slip a few days ago and asked her not to go. She hadn't thought he was serous. He had been serious. Unfortunately, he and Trinity didn't have the kind of relationship where he could ask her to stay.

Then change it.

He frowned, wondering where the heck that thought

had come from. Before he could dwell on it any longer, the sound of Trinity's voice broke into his thoughts.

"This is a beautiful place, Adrian. Dinner was fabulous. Thanks for bringing me here."

He smiled at her. "Glad you approve."

"I do. And the past two weeks with you have been wonderful, as well. I needed them."

He'd needed them, as well, for several reasons. His eyes had opened to a number of things. She had become very important to him. "Want to dance?"

"I'd love to."

As he led her onto the dance floor he thought of their other nights together. Lazy. Non-rushed. Just what the two of them needed. Usually on workdays they got together during the evenings. They would order out for dinner or settle in with grilled-cheese sandwiches. Once or twice he'd brought work from the office and while she stretched out on the sofa reading some medical journal or another, he would stretch out on the floor with his laptop.

He was aware of her every movement. She felt comfortable around him and he felt comfortable around her. She had allowed him into her space and he had allowed her into his. He'd never shared this kind of closeness with any woman. Frankly, he'd figured he never could. She'd proved him wrong.

And their mornings together had been equally special. He would wake up with her naked body pressed against his after a night of nearly nonstop lovemaking. Usually he woke before she did and would wait patiently for her eyes to open. And when they did, he welcomed her to a new day with a kiss meant to curl her toes.

That kiss would lead to other things, prompting them to christen the day in a wonderful way, a way that fueled his energy for the rest of the day.

And she would soon be leaving.

"How did the meeting with your family go?"

He had mentioned Rico's investigation, and this morning before they had parted he had told her that a meeting had been called. He gazed into her beautiful features as he held her in his arms on the dance floor. He told her everything that Rico had uncovered.

"At least now you know the part all four women played in your great-grandfather's life. I guess the next step is finding those other Westmorelands, the ones from the son Raphel never knew he had. The Outlaws."

"Yes. I think Raphel would want that. My great-grandfather went out of his way to help others. He was an extraordinary man."

"So is his great-grandson Adrian. You went out of you way to help me."

"For what good it did."

"It doesn't matter. You still did it. And I will always appreciate you for trying." She placed her head on his chest and he tightened his arms around her.

Moments later, she lifted her eyes to his and the combination of her beauty, her scent and the entrancing music from a live band made the sexual awareness between them even more potent. As if on cue, they moved closer. The feel of her hands on his shoulders sent heat spiraling through him.

The tips of her breasts hardened against his chest, something not even the material of his shirt could conceal. Wordlessly they danced, his gaze silently telling her just what he wanted, what he would be getting later.

To make sure she fully understood, he moved his fingertips down the curve of her spine. He drew slow circles in the spot he'd discovered was one of her erogenous zones. Whenever he placed a kiss in the small of her back she would come undone. Already he felt her trembling in his arms.

He leaned down, close to her ear. "Ready to leave?"

She answered on a breathless sigh. "Yes."

He led her off the dance floor.

Trinity didn't have to wonder what was happening to her. She was having an Adrian Westmoreland moment. Nothing new for her. But for some reason, tonight was more intense than ever before.

She could attribute it to a number of things. The romantic atmosphere of the restaurant, the delicious food they'd eaten or the handsome man who was whisking through traffic to get her home. From the moment Adrian had picked her up for dinner, he had been attentive, charming and more sexually appealing than any man had a right to be.

All through dinner she had watched him watching her. The buildup of sexual awareness had been slow and deliberate. She'd discovered Westmoreland men had a certain kind of charisma and there was nothing any woman could do about it. Except enjoy it.

And she had. All through dinner she had known she was the object of his fascination. He had captivated her with an appeal that wouldn't be denied. Now, as far as she was concerned, they couldn't get back to her place fast enough.

It was then that she noticed they weren't returning to her home. Otherwise, he would have gotten off the interstate exits ago. He was taking her to his place.

She glanced over at him, and as if reading her thoughts, he briefly took his gaze off the road. "I want you in *my* bed."

His words made her already hot body that much hotter. She gave him a smile. "Does it matter whose bed?"

"Tonight it does."

She was still pondering his response when he opened the door to his condo a few minutes later. Usually, whenever she visited Adrian's place, she took in the view of the majestic beauty of the surrounding mountains. But not tonight.

Tonight, her entire focus was on one man.

He closed the door behind them, locking them in. He beckoned her with his eyes, mesmerizing her. He was challenging her in a way she'd never been challenged before. And it wasn't all physical. Why was he going after the emotional, as well?

Before she could give that question any more thought, he began moving toward her in slow, deliberate steps. As she watched him, a rush of heat raced through her. The look in his eyes was intense, hypnotic, gripping.

When he stopped in front of her, undefinable feelings bombarded her. She'd never felt this way before, at least not to this degree. She reached out and pushed the jacket from his shoulders.

And then she kissed him all over his face while unbuttoning his shirt. An inner voice told her to slow down, but she couldn't. Their time together was limited. When her transfer was approved she would be leaving. Within hours, if she had her way. She'd already begun packing, telling herself the sooner Denver was behind her the better. But now she wasn't so sure. She had that one nagging doubt... only because of Adrian.

When she reached for his belt, he said, "Let me."

So she did, watching as he stripped off the rest of his clothes before he turned and stripped off hers. Then he carried her into the bedroom.

There was something about his lovemaking tonight that stirred everything inside her. His kisses were demanding, his hands strong yet gentle. His tongue licked every inch of her body, reducing her to a mass of trembling need.

When she thought she couldn't possibly endure any more of his foreplay and survive, he entered her, thrusting deeper than she thought possible. He looked down into her eyes and she felt something…she wasn't sure what. In response, she cupped his face in her hand. "Make me scream."

He did more than that. Before it was over, she'd clawed his back and left her teeth prints on his shoulder. She was totally undone. Out of control. His thrusts were powerful and her hips moved in rhythm with his strokes, in perfect sync.

Over and over he brought her to the brink of ecstasy, then he'd deliberately snatch her back. His finger inched up toward that particular area of her back and she let out a moan knowing what was about to come.

"Now!"

With his husky command, her body exploded and she ground against his manhood as she screamed his name. It seemed her scream spurred him to greater heights because his thrusts became even more forceful.

He threw his head back and his body began quivering with his own orgasm. She felt the thick richness of his release jutting through her entire body. She was suddenly stunned by the force of need that overtook her, made her come again as he once again carried her to great heights from this world and beyond.

Moments later when she slumped against him, weak as water, limp as a noodle, she knew her world would not be the same without him in it.

Nineteen

"You're looking rather well, Dr. Matthews."

Trinity's skin crawled. She'd known when she arrived at work this morning that her and Dr. Belvedere's paths would cross. This was his first day back at the hospital since returning to the city. She just hadn't expected him to approach her so soon. It wasn't even ten o'clock. She was wearing the necklace recorder and it was set.

"Thank you, Dr. Belvedere. I take it your trip to Texas went well."

"Of course it did. But what I want to know about is this foolishness I've heard. You've put in for a transfer?"

"Yes, sir, you heard correctly. More than once over the past six months you've made unwanted advances toward me. I've told you I'm not interested, and that I'm already involved with someone. Yet you refuse to accept my words. I feel I have no choice but to work at another hospital."

A smile touched his features. "Yes, you've made it clear that you're not interested in sleeping with me, but it doesn't matter what you want, Doctor. It's all about what I want, which is to engage in a sexual relationship with you. Only then will I be satisfied enough to let you continue your work here."

Trinity wanted him to make things perfectly clear...for the record. "Are you saying you will never let me do my job here unless I sleep with you?"

"That's precisely what I'm saying, Dr. Matthews. And it won't do you any good to report me. No one will say anything to me. They need that children's wing and my family is making sure they get it. You should consider our little tryst something for the cause. You'll be doing all those sick kiddies a favor."

"I refuse to believe there is no one here at the hospital who will put you in check."

He chuckled. "Believe it. It doesn't matter who you talk to. I am a Belvedere and I do as I please. Haven't you learned that yet?"

"I refuse to be sexually harassed, which is why I put in for that transfer."

"Unfortunately you won't be getting it. I talked to Dr. Fowler this morning and he agrees with me. Your transfer will be denied."

Anger flared within Trinity. "You can't do that. I am a good doctor."

"I can and I will. And as far as being a good doctor, show up at my place tonight and prove just how *good* you are. Seven o'clock sharp and don't be late. I'll even leave the door unlocked for you. Just find your way to my bedroom and come prepared to stay all night. I've already arranged for you to have tomorrow off. You're going to need it." Then he turned and walked away with a smug look on his face.

It took Trinity a while to gather her composure. Telling one of the other doctors that she wasn't feeling well and needed to leave for the rest of the day, she caught the elevator to the parking garage. As soon as she was inside her car she called Rico. "I think I have what we need to nail Dr. Belvedere."

* * *

Trinity called Adrian and he met her at Rico's office where the three of them listened to the recording of Belvedere's conversation with her. It took all of Adrian's effort to contain his anger.

"Well, you're right. This will nail him," Rico said, fighting back his anger, as well. "He'll willingly give you that transfer to keep this recording out of anyone's hands."

"But it shouldn't be that easy for him," Adrian snapped, unable to restrain the rage he felt. "What about other women after Trinity? How long will it take before he's hitting on another woman? Forcing her to do sexual favors against her will? Do you honestly think getting his hand spanked for coming on to Trinity will make much difference?"

Rico met Adrian's gaze. "No. But unless Trinity is willing to go public by filing a sexual harassment lawsuit, there's nothing else we can do."

Adrian turned to Trinity. "Are you willing to do that?"

She shook her head. "No, Adrian. At this point all I want is my transfer. I don't have the money to go against him and I could ruin my reputation and my medical career if I were to lose the case. I don't want to even imagine the legal fees. Even with this recording, I doubt fighting it will do any good. His family has too much power."

Adrian glanced over at Rico who shrugged. "The Belvederes do have power, Adrian. And it seems they have been allowed to get away with stuff for so long, it will merely be a matter of buying off certain people. I agree with Trinity, there is a risk she might be forced to stop practicing medicine while the case is resolved, which might take some time. Unless…"

Adrian's brow lifted. "Unless what?"

"Unless we called them out in such a way where they would have no choice but to make sure Belvedere never practices medicine again."

"Strip him of his medical license?" Trinity asked.

"Yes."

She sucked in a deep breath. "It won't happen. His family won't allow it. Right or wrong, they will still back him. In the end they will get what they want."

Trinity stood. "All I want is my transfer to be approved and after listening to that tape I'm certain the hospital administrators won't allow Dr. Belvedere to block it. If they do, then I'll go public."

"I never took you for a quitter, Trinity."

She lifted her chin. She'd known the moment Adrian walked into her house that he was still upset with her. After the meeting with Rico ended, he'd barely said two words.

"You think I'm a quitter because I won't take what Dr. Belvedere did public?"

"Yes. By not doing so you're letting him get away, letting him do the same thing to other women. You have the ability to stop him now."

"That's where you're wrong, Adrian. You heard what Rico said. Going against that family is useless. In the end—"

"You'll risk hurting your medical career. I know. I heard him. Is your career all you can think about?"

His question set a spark off within her. How dare he judge her? "No, it's not all I can think about, Adrian," she said, angry that he would think such a thing. "It's not about me but about the children."

"What children?"

"The sick kids who really need that wing the Belvederes are building. You heard what he said in that recording. If I make waves, they will withdraw their funding."

Adrian stared at her. "The way you're thinking is no better than those administrators at Denver Memorial. They are willing to turn a blind eye to what's going on to keep money rolling in."

"Yes, it's all politics, Adrian. That's the way it's played. It's not fair but—"

"It won't stop until someone takes a stand, Trinity. He was trying to force you into his bed. He expects you to show up at his place tonight. And then he has the gall to give you tomorrow off like he's doing you a damn favor. How can you let him get away with that?"

"He's not getting away with it."

"Yes, he is. All you're doing is demanding that he not block that transfer so you can haul ass from here."

Anger erupted within her. "Yes, I want to leave Denver. Why do you have a problem with that? If I make a fuss the hospital will lose a needed pediatric wing and I could have a ruined career. All you're thinking about is losing a bed partner, Adrian."

He took a step toward her. "You think that's all you are to me, Trinity? Well, you're wrong. I've fallen in love with you. I didn't realize it until I listened to that recording. As I sat there, all I could think about was that jerk disrespecting you. You are a woman whose body I've loved and cherished for the past month. But he only considers you a sex object for his own personal satisfaction."

"You've fallen in love with me?" she asked, not believing she'd heard him right.

"Yes. I hadn't planned to tell you since I know I'm not included in your dreams and goals. But even knowing that, I couldn't stop falling in love with you anyway. Imagine that." Without saying anything else he walked out the door.

Adrian was so angry he couldn't see straight. As far as he was concerned Casey Belvedere had crossed the line big time, and the idea of him getting away with it, or not getting the punishment he deserved, made even more rage flare through him

Trinity was such a dedicated doctor that her concern was for the children who needed that new wing. As far as Adrian was concerned, the Belvedere name didn't deserve to be attached to the hospital anyway. It wasn't as if they were the only people with money.

That last thought had ideas running through Adrian's head. He checked his watch. It was just a little after noon. He decided to run his idea by Dillon and hopefully things would take off from there.

"Adrian actually told you he's fallen in love with you?" Tara asked her sister. "Evidently you forgot to tell me a few things along the way. I wasn't aware things had gotten serious between the two of you."

Trinity sighed. She hadn't told her sister about becoming Adrian's real lover. "If by getting serious you mean sleeping together, then yes. That started weeks ago and we had an understanding. No promises and no expectations."

Trinity started from the beginning and told Tara everything. "So how could he fall in love with me? He knows I hate big cities. He knows I planned to leave Denver after I completed residency. He likes outdoorsy stuff and I don't. He—"

"Don't you know that opposites attract?" Tara asked her. "And when it comes to love, sometimes we fall in love with the person we least expect. Lord knows I had no intention of losing my heart to Thorn, and if you were to ask him, he probably felt the same way about me in the beginning."

Trinity couldn't imagine such a thing. First, she couldn't envision any woman not falling head-over-heels for her handsome brother-in-law. Second, Thorn adored Tara and Trinity refused to believe it hadn't always been that way.

"Well, I have no intention of falling in love with anyone

and I don't want any man to fall in love with me. My career in medicine is all I want."

"I used to think that way, too, at one time, especially after that incident with Derrick," Tara said. "Having a solid career is nice, but there's nothing like sharing your life with someone you can trust, someone you know will always have your back. There's no reason you can't have both, a career and the love of a good man."

"But I don't want both."

"Who are you trying to convince, Trinity? Me or yourself?"

Trinity nervously gnawed her bottom lip. Instead of answering Tara, she said, "I need to go. Canyon's wife, Keisha, offered to be at the meeting at the hospital in the morning and represent me. I need to call her to go over a few things."

"Okay. Take care of your business. And…Trinity?"

"Yes."

"Having a man love you has its merits. You loving him back is definitely a plus."

Adrian spent the rest of the day at the office making calls as he tried to pull his plan together. It wasn't as easy as he originally thought it would be. Most of his friends were in debt repaying student loans. That meant reaching out to family members who were known philanthropists such as Thorn, his cousin Delaney, whose husband was a sheikh, and their cousin Jared, who was a renowned divorce attorney representing a number of celebrities.

Adrian was about to get an international connection to call Delaney in the Middle East when the phone rang. "This is Adrian."

"I've got everything arranged and everyone can attend the meeting. We can meet at McKays," Dillon said.

Adrian glanced at his watch. "Can we make it at eight? I have somewhere to be at seven."

"Okay. Eight o'clock will work."

"Thanks, Dil. I appreciate it."

Adrian really meant it. Dillon had contacted the board members of the Westmoreland Foundation, a charity organization his family had established to honor the memory of his parents, aunt and uncle. Usually the foundation's main focuses were scholarships and cancer research. Dillon had arranged a meeting with everyone so Adrian could present a proposal to add a children's hospital wing to the list.

He glanced at his watch again and then stood to put on his jacket. It was a little after six. His seven o'clock meeting was one he didn't intend to miss.

At exactly seven o'clock, Adrian walked into Dr. Casey Belvedere's home. The man had left the door unlocked just as he'd told Trinity he would do. Adrian glanced around the lavishly decorated house. At any other time he would have paused to appreciate the décor, but not now and certainly not today.

"You're on time. I'm upstairs waiting," a voice called out.

Without responding, Adrian took off his jacket and neatly placed it across the arm of one of the chairs. He then took his time walking up the huge spiral staircase.

"I've been waiting on you," Belvedere said. "I'm going to give you a treat."

Adrian stepped into the bedroom and discovered Belvedere sprawled across the bed naked. The man's eyes almost popped out of his head when he saw Adrian, and he quickly jumped up and grabbed for his robe.

"What the hell are you doing here? You're trespassing. I'm calling the police."

Ignoring his threat, Adrian moved forward and said, "You disrespected *my* woman for the last time."

Before Belvedere could react, Adrian connected his fist to the man's jaw, sending the man falling backward onto the bed. Adrian then reached for Belvedere and gave him a hard jab in the stomach, followed by a brutal right hook to the side of his face. After a few more blows, he took the bottle of champagne chilling in the bucket and broke the bottle against the bedpost. He tossed the remaining liquid onto Belvedere's face to keep him from passing out.

"Go ahead and call the police—I dare you. If I have to deal with them, I'll make sure the next time I break every one of your damn fingers. Let's see how well you can perform surgery after that."

Adrian left, grabbing his jacket on the way out, and silently thanking Aidan for convincing him to take boxing classes in college.

Twenty

Trinity pulled herself up in bed and ran her fingers through her hair. She couldn't sleep. Her meeting with Keisha had taken its toll on her. They'd covered every legal aspect of the meeting they'd planned to spring on Dr. Belvedere and the hospital administration tomorrow. The element of surprise was on their side and Keisha intended to keep it that way.

Another reason Trinity couldn't sleep was that this was the first time in several weeks that she'd slept alone. She had gotten used to cuddling up to Adrian's warm, muscular body. He would hold her during the night while his chin rested on the crown of her head. She hadn't realized how safe and secure she'd felt while he was with her until now.

She glanced at the clock on her nightstand before easing out of bed. It was not even midnight yet. Keisha had instructed her not to go into work tomorrow. As her attorney, Keisha would call the hospital and request an appointment with the hospital administrator, asking that the hospital attorney, Dr. Fowler, and Dr. Belvedere be present. Just from talking to Keisha, Trinity could tell the woman was a shrewd attorney. Trinity couldn't wait to see how Keisha pulled things off.

When Trinity walked into her kitchen she realized how

empty the room seemed. Adrian had made his presence known in every room of her house and she was missing him like crazy.

If I'm feeling this way about him now, then how will I cope after moving miles and miles away from here?

"I'll cope," she muttered to herself as she set her coffeemaker into motion. "He's just a man."

Then a sharp pain hit her in the chest, right below her heart. He wasn't just a man. He was a man who loved her. A man who had been willing to let her go, to let her leave Denver to pursue her dreams and goals.

Sitting down at the kitchen table, she sipped her coffee, thinking of all the memories they'd made in this very room. Adrian cooking omelets in the middle of the night; them sharing a bowl of ice cream; them making love on this table, against the refrigerator, in the chair and on the counter when they should have been loading the dishwasher.

She knew all the other rooms in her house had similar memories, and those memories wouldn't end once she left Denver. They would remain with her permanently. At that moment she knew why.

She had fallen in love with him.

Trinity sighed as a single tear fell down her cheek. She tried to imagine life without Adrian and couldn't. No matter where she went or what she did, she would long for him, want to be with him, want to share her life with him. What Tara had said earlier was true. *Having a man love you has its merits, but you loving him back is definitely a plus.*

Wiping the tear from her eye, Trinity stood and headed for her bedroom. Adrian was angry with her. He thought she was a quitter. She intended to prove him wrong. This wasn't just about her. Those kids deserved better than a hospital wing from benefactors who routinely abused power.

After talking to Keisha and thinking about what Adrian had said, Trinity had changed her mind. It wasn't just about getting her transfer approved anymore. She knew that Dr. Belvedere had to go, and he could take Dr. Fowler and all those other hospital administrators who had turned a blind eye right along with him. If it meant she had to take them on, then she would do it because she knew she had Adrian backing her up. That meant everything to her.

She picked up the phone. It was late but Keisha had told her to call at any time since she would be up working on the logistics for tomorrow's meeting.

Trinity's conversation with Keisha lasted a few minutes. She quickly stripped off her nightgown, slid into a dress and was out the door.

Adrian was soaking his knuckles and thinking about Trinity. What would she say when she found out what he'd done to Belvedere tonight? As far as Adrian was concerned, the man had gotten just what he deserved. Every time Adrian remembered walking into that bedroom finding Belvedere naked and waiting for Trinity to arrive, Adrian wished he could have gotten in more punches.

He had no regrets about admitting that he loved Trinity. It had been as much a revelation to him as it was to her, but he did love her and the thought of her leaving Denver was a pain he knew he would have to bear. She didn't love him and her future plans did not include him. Now he understood how Aidan had felt when things had ended between him and Jillian. Evidently he and his twin were destined to be the recipients of broken hearts.

Aidan had called Adrian when he'd left Belvedere's place. His brother had been concerned when he felt Adrian's anger. Adrian had assured Aidan he was okay. He had handled some business he should have taken care of weeks ago.

The meeting with Dillon, his brothers and cousins had gone well and they'd unanimously agreed to shift some of the donation dollars toward the hospital if the need arose. Adrian knew from Canyon that Trinity was using Keisha as her attorney and they planned to meet with Belvedere and the hospital administrators tomorrow. Adrian would do just about anything to be a fly on the wall at that meeting to see Belvedere in the hot seat trying to explain what he'd said on that recording.

The police hadn't arrived to arrest Adrian, which meant Belvedere had taken his threat to heart. Um, then again, maybe not, Adrian thought when he heard the sound of his doorbell. It was late and he wasn't expecting anyone. If it was the police, he would deal with them. He had no regrets about what he'd done to Belvedere. At this point, he wasn't even concerned about Dillon finding out about what he'd done.

He glanced out the peephole to make sure Belvedere hadn't sent goons to work him over. His breath caught hard in his chest. It was Trinity. Had Belvedere done something crazy and sought some kind of revenge on her instead of coming after him?

He quickly opened the door. "Trinity? Are you okay?"

A nervous smile framed her lips. "That depends on you, Adrian."

Not sure what she meant by that, he moved aside. "Come on in and let's talk."

Lordy, did Adrian always have to smell so nice? Trinity could feel heat emitting from him. At least he was wearing clothes—jeans riding low on his hips. But he wasn't wearing a shirt and it didn't take much for her to recall the number of times she had licked that chest.

"Can I get you something to drink?"

She turned around and swallowed as her gaze took in all of him. She must not have been thinking with a full deck to even consider leaving him behind.

"Coffee, if you have it. I started on a cup at my place but never finished it."

"A cup of coffee coming up. I could use one myself. We can drink it in here or you can join me in the kitchen."

His kitchen held as many hot and steamy memories as her own. That might be a good place to start her groveling. "The kitchen is fine."

She followed him and, as usual, she appreciated how his backside filled out his jeans. She took a seat at the table. She knew her way around his kitchen as much as he knew his way around hers, although hers was a lot smaller.

Trinity noticed the magazine on the table, one that contained house floor plans and architectural designs. He had mentioned a couple of weeks ago that he would start building on his property in Westmoreland Country sometime next year. She picked up the magazine and browsed through it, noticing several plans he had highlighted.

He had started the coffeemaker and was leaning back against the counter staring at her. Instant attraction thickened her lungs and made it difficult to swallow. She broke eye contact with him. Moments later she looked back at him and he was still staring.

"Nice magazine," she somehow found the voice to say. "You're thinking of building your home sooner than planned?"

He shrugged massive shoulders. "After you leave I figured I needed to do something to keep myself busy for a while. I was thinking that might do it."

She didn't say anything as she looked back at one of the designs he had marked. "I see you marked a few."

"Yes. I marked a few."

When she glanced back at him he had turned to the counter to pour coffee into their cups. She let out a sigh of relief. She doubted she could handle staring into his penetrating dark gaze right now. It would be nice if he put on a shirt, but this was his house and he could do as he pleased. It wasn't his fault she had stocked up a lot of fantasies about his chest.

She turned back to the designs. All the ones he had highlighted were nice; most were double stories and huge. But then all the Westmorelands had huge homes on their properties.

"Here you go," he said, setting the cups of coffee on the table. That's when she noticed his knuckles. They were bruised.

She grabbed his arm, glancing up at him. "What happened to your hands?"

"Nothing."

She let go of his arm and he sat across from her at the table. Her forehead crunched into a frown. How could he say that nothing had happened when she could clearly see that something had?

"What happened to your hands, Adrian?" she asked again. "Did you injure yourself?"

A slight smile touched his features. "No, I did a little boxing."

She lifted a brow. "You can box?"

He nodded as he took a sip of his coffee. "Yes. Aidan and I took it up in college. We were both on Harvard's boxing team."

"Oh." She took a sip of her own coffee. "And you boxed today without any gloves?"

"Yes. I didn't have them with me."

Before she could ask him anything else, he had a question of his own. "So what's going on with you that depends on me, Trinity?"

She placed her coffee cup down, staring into those deep, dark, penetrating eyes. She hoped what she had to say didn't come too late. "Earlier today you said you have fallen in love with me."

He nodded slowly as he continued to hold her gaze. "Yes, I said it."

"You meant it?"

His lips firmed. "I've told you before that I never say anything I don't mean. Yes, I love you. To be honest with you, I didn't see it coming. I wasn't expecting to fall in love, and only realized the extent of my feelings today."

She nodded. What he'd just said was perfect. "In that case, hopefully you won't find what I'm about to tell you odd." She covered one of his hands with hers, being careful of his bruised knuckles. "I love you, too, Adrian. And to be quite honest, I didn't see it coming, I wasn't expecting it and only today—after you left—did I realize the full extent of my feelings."

She watched his entire body tense as he continued to stare into her eyes. Realizing he needed another affirmation, she tightened her hold on his hand and said, with all the love pouring from her heart, "I love you, Adrian Westmoreland."

She wasn't sure how he moved so quickly, but he was out of his chair and had pulled her into his lap before she could respond. Then he was kissing her as though he never intended to stop. A part of her hoped he didn't.

But eventually they had to come up for air. She cupped his face, fighting back tears. "I will remain in Denver with you. Not sure if I'll have a job after tomorrow, but I will be here with you."

"So you won't be leaving?" he asked as if he had to make sure he had heard her correctly.

Trinity smiled. "And leave my heart behind? No way." She paused. "You were right. The children at that hospital deserve a competent staff as much as they deserve a hospital wing. I've already talked to Keisha. I want more than just a guarantee that I'll get that transfer to another hospital. I want to clean house.

"So you might want to think about whether or not you want to have your name linked with mine. I plan to go public with everything Casey Belvedere has done unless he and the hospital administrators agree to leave voluntarily."

Adrian tightened his arms around her. "Don't worry about our names being linked. I am proud of your decision and support you one hundred percent. The entire Westmoreland family does." He then told her of the meeting he'd had with Dillon and his family earlier that day.

More tears came into her eyes as she realized that even when he hadn't known she loved him, he had gone to his family to do that for her. As she'd told him a few days ago, he was an extraordinary man just as Raphel had been.

"Don't worry about how tomorrow will go down. I will be there by your side."

She leaned up and placed a kiss on his lips. "Thank you."

He held her in his arms as if he knew that's what she needed. "When did you realize that you love me?" he asked her.

She looked up at him. "Tonight. When I woke up and you weren't there. I missed you, but I knew it was more than just the physical. I missed the mental, as well. The emotional. I also realized that even if I got the transfer I couldn't endure being separated from you. I knew I wanted a future with you as much as I wanted a career in medicine and that it didn't matter where I lived as long as we were together. You, Adrian Westmoreland, are my dream."

Adrian's features filled with so much emotion that his look almost brought tears to Trinity's eyes.

He crushed her to his chest, whispering, "I love you so damn much, Trinity. It scares me."

She tightened her arms around him and said softly, "Not as much as it scares me. But we'll be fine. Together we're going to make it."

Deep in her heart she knew that they would.

Twenty-One

The next morning Trinity glanced around the hospital's huge conference room. Keisha was seated on her left, Adrian on her right. Dillon sat beside Adrian and a man Keisha had introduced as Stan Harmer, the hospital commissioner of Colorado, sat beside Keisha. Mr. Harmer was responsible for the operations of all hospitals in the state and just happened to be in Denver when Adrian had called him that morning. Things worked out in Adrian's favor because it just so happened that the man was a huge fan of Thorn's.

"You okay?" Adrian asked Trinity.

"It would have been nice to have gotten a little more sleep last night."

He chuckled. "Baby, you got just what you asked for."

She smiled. Yes, she couldn't deny that.

At that moment the conference room door opened and a stocky man, probably Anthony Oats, the hospital's attorney, walked in, followed by Dr. Fowler, who almost stumbled when he recognized Stan Harmer. Both men uttered a quick, "Good morning," before hurrying to their seats.

Trinity noticed that Wendell Fowler refused to look at her. Instead, once seated, he bowed his head and said something to Anthony Oats who chuckled loudly and then glanced her way.

"Don't worry about what's going on across the table," Keisha whispered to Trinity. "They are playing mind games while trying to figure out what we might have other than your word against theirs. They are pretty confident you don't have anything."

Trinity nodded and when she glanced up she saw the man she had met last month, Roger Belvedere, Dr. Casey Belvedere's brother, enter the room. She was surprised to see him. She could tell by the others' expressions that she wasn't the only one.

"Why is Roger Belvedere attending our meeting?" Anthony Oats asked, standing. "This is a private hospital matter."

Keisha smiled sweetly. "Not really, Mr. Oats. And since it could possibly involve the completion of the hospital wing bearing his family's name, I felt it would be nice to include him. So I called this morning and invited him. Besides, there's a chance Mr. Belvedere might be our next governor," she added for good measure, mainly to flatter the man.

Roger Belvedere beamed, and Trinity knew he didn't have a clue what the meeting would be about. He took a seat at the table and glanced around the room. "Where's my brother?" he asked the chief of pediatrics, who suddenly seemed a little nervous.

Dr. Fowler cleared his throat a few times before answering. "He wasn't aware of this meeting until this morning. He wasn't scheduled to work today."

"I wonder why," Trinity heard Adrian mutter under his breath.

"I understand he needed to stop by his physician's office. It seems he was in some sort of accident last night."

Roger raised a brow. "Really? I didn't know that. It must

not have been too serious or he would have contacted the family."

At that moment, the conference room door opened and Casey Belvedere walked in at a slow pace. Trinity gasped, and she wasn't the only one. The man's face looked as though it had been hit by a truck.

Roger was out of his seat in a flash. "What the hell happened to you?" he asked his brother.

"Accident," Belvedere muttered through a swollen jaw. He then looked at everyone around the table. Trinity noticed that the moment he saw Adrian, fear leaped into his eyes.

Trinity wasn't the only one who noticed the reaction. Dillon noticed it, as well, and both his and Trinity's gazes shifted from Dr. Belvedere to Adrian, who managed to keep a straight face. Trinity suddenly knew the cause of Adrian's bruised knuckles and she had a feeling Dillon knew, as well. Adrian had gone boxing, all right, and there was no doubt in her mind with whom.

Dr. Belvedere looked over at Dr. Fowler. "What's going on here? Why was I called to this meeting on my day off? Who are all these people and what is Roger doing here?"

It was Keisha who spoke. "Please have a seat, Dr. Belvedere, so we can get started. I promise to explain everything."

He glared across the table at Keisha as he took a seat. And then the meeting began.

Casey Belvedere was furious. "Surely none of you are going to take the word of this resident over mine. It's apparent she's nothing more than an opportunist. Evidently Mr. Westmoreland doesn't have enough money for her, so she wants to go after my family's wealth."

It took every ounce of Trinity's control not to say anything while Belvedere made all sorts of derogatory comments about her character. Keisha would pat her on the thigh under the table, signaling her to keep her cool. Trinity in turn would do the same to Adrian. She swore she could hear the blood boiling inside him.

At the beginning, when Keisha had introduced everyone present, she had surprised Trinity by introducing Adrian as Trinity's fiancé and Dillon as a family friend.

"I agree with Dr. Belvedere," Anthony Oaks said, smiling. "Mr. Belvedere and his brother are stellar members of our community. It's unfortunate that Dr. Matthews has targeted their family for her little drama. Unless you have concrete proof of—"

"We do," Keisha said, smiling.

Trinity immediately saw surprise leap into both men's eyes.

"Just what kind of proof?" Roger Belvedere asked, indignation in his tone. "My family and I are proud of the family's name. As the eldest grandson of Langley and Melinda Belvedere, I don't intend for anyone to impugn our honor for financial gain."

"You tell them, Roger," Casey Belvedere said.

Keisha merely gave both men a smooth smile. "My client has kept a journal where she has recorded each and every incident…even those she reported to Dr. Fowler where nothing was done." Keisha slid the thick binder to the center of the table.

"And we're supposed to believe whatever she wrote in that?" Mr. Oats said, laughing as if the entire thing was a joke.

Keisha's gaze suddenly became razor sharp. "No. But I'm sure you will believe this," she said, placing a mini recorder in front of her. She clicked it on and the room grew silent as everyone listened, stunned.

Although he'd heard the recording before, listening to it fired up Adrian's blood over again. This was the first time

Dillon had heard it and Adrian could tell from his cousin's expression that his blood was fired up, as well.

"Turn that damn thing off!" Dr. Belvedere shouted. "That's not me, I tell you. They dubbed my voice."

Keisha smiled. "I figured you would claim that."

She then passed around the table a document on FBI letterhead. "I had your voice tested for authentication, Dr. Belvedere, and that is your voice. For the past six to eight months you have done nothing but create a hostile work environment for my client. We didn't have to request this meeting. We could have taken this recording straight to the media."

"But you didn't," Roger Belvedere said, looking at his brother in disgust. "That means you want a monetary settlement. How much? Name your price."

Adrian shook his head sadly. The Belvederes were used to buying their way out of situations. It was sickening. But they wouldn't be able to do that this time, at least not the way they expected. Keisha was good and she was going for blood.

Again Keisha smiled. "Our *price* just might surprise you."

Adrian leaned back in his chair and inwardly smiled. He reached beneath the table and gripped Trinity's hand in his, sending a silent message that things would be okay. The Belvederes would discover the hard way that this was one show they wouldn't be running.

Wordlessly, Adrian opened the door to his home and pulled Trinity into his arms. This had been a taxing day and he was glad to see it over.

Dr. Casey Belvedere would no longer be allowed to practice medicine. He was barred not only in the State of Colorado, but also in any other state, for three years. In addition, he would go through extensive therapy. The Belvedere name would be removed from the hospital wing, but their funding would remain intact.

Dr. Wendell Fowler had been relieved of his duties. In fact, Stan Harmer had pretty much fired him right there on the spot and indicated that Dr. Fowler would not be managing another medical facility in the State of Colorado. Further, sexual harassment training would be required of all hospital staff.

To top it off, a sexual harassment suit would be filed against Dr. Belvedere and the hospital. Roger Belvedere hadn't taken that well since it would be a scandal that would affect his campaign for governor. More details would be worked out.

The money Trinity would get if she settled out of court would be enough to build her own medical complex for children, right here in Denver. But first she had to get through her residency. Her transfer was approved right after the meeting by Stan Harmer, and she had her pick of any area hospital. The man had also said Colorado needed more doctors like her. Doctors with integrity who put their patients before their own selfish needs.

She'd been given a month off with pay to rest up mentally after the ordeal Dr. Belvedere had put her through. Keisha had refused to accept Roger Belvedere's suggestion that everything be handled privately and kept from the media. She had let him know that she would be calling the shots and they would be playing by her rules.

Now, Trinity gazed into Adrian's eyes and his love stirred sensations within her.

"I want you," he whispered as he proceeded to remove her clothes.

Then he removed his own clothes and carried her up the stairs to his bedroom. Standing her beside the bed, he kissed her, tenderly, thoroughly, full of the passion she had come to expect from him.

"I want to take you to your home in Florida," he told her softly, placing small kisses around her lips. "This weekend."

"Why?"

"Don't you think it's time I met your parents? Plus, I want your father to know all my intentions toward his daughter are honorable."

She tilted her head back to look up at him. "Are they?"

"Yes. I want to ask his permission to marry you."

Trinity's heart stopped beating as happiness raced through her. "You want to marry me?"

He chuckled. "Yes. I guess we'll have to get in line behind Stern and JoJo, though. But before the year ends, I want you to be Mrs. Adrian Westmoreland. No more pretenses of any kind. We're going for the real thing, making it legal."

He kissed her again. Tonight was theirs and she intended to scream it away.

Epilogue

"Stern, you may kiss your bride."

Cheers went up when Stern took JoJo in his arms. Sitting in the audience, Trinity had a hard time keeping a dry eye. JoJo looked beautiful and when she'd walked down the aisle toward Stern, Trinity could feel the love between them.

The wedding was held in the Rocky Mountains at Stern's hunting lodge. However, today, thanks to Riley's wife, Alpha, who was an event planner, the lodge had been transformed into a wedding paradise. It was totally breathtaking. Stern and JoJo had wanted an outdoor wedding and felt their favorite getaway spot was the perfect place. Trinity had to agree.

"Miss me?" a deep, male voice whispered in her ear as she stood at one of the buffet tables. Adrian and all of his Denver cousins and brothers had been groomsmen in the wedding.

Trinity turned and smiled. Then her smile was replaced with a frown. "Hey, wait a minute. You aren't Adrian."

The man quirked a brow, grinning. "You sure?"

Trinity grinned back. "Positive. So where is my husband-to-be?"

"He sent me to find you. Told me to tell you he's waiting down by the pond."

"Okay."

Trinity saw Aidan's eyes fill with emotion as he stared across the yard. She followed the direction of his gaze to where Pam and her three younger sisters stood. Trinity had met the women a few weeks ago when they'd come home to try on their bridal dresses. She thought Jillian, Nadia and Paige were beautiful, just like their older sister.

"Aidan? Is anything wrong?" Trinity asked him, concerned.

He looked back at her and gave her a small smile. "No, nothing's wrong. Excuse me for a minute." She watched as he quickly walked off.

It took Trinity longer than she expected to reach the pond. Several people had stopped to congratulate her on her engagement. Most had admired the gorgeous ring Adrian had placed on her finger a few months ago. They would be getting married in August in her hometown of Bunnell. They planned to live in Adrian's condo while their home in Westmoreland Country—Adrian's Cove—was under construction.

She found her intended, standing by the pond, waiting for her. He held open his arms and she raced to him, feeling as happy as any woman could be. He leaned down and kissed her.

"Happy?" he asked, smiling down at her.

"Very much so," she said returning his smile. And she truly meant it.

Once the details of the sexual harassment lawsuit had gone public, the Belvederes, not surprisingly, hired a high-profile attorney who tried to claim his client was innocent. That attempt fell through, however, when other women began coming forward with their own accusations of sexual harassment. So far there were a total of twelve in all. Keisha expected more.

Casey Belvedere was no longer practicing medicine, and Roger Belvedere had withdrawn his name as a gubernatorial candidate. Consumers and women's advocacy groups were boycotting all Belvedere dairy products. Needless to say, over the past few months, the family had taken a huge financial hit.

Adrian took Trinity's hand in his and they began walking around the pond. He needed a quiet moment with the woman he loved. The past three months had been hectic as hell. They had flown to Florida where he had asked Frank Matthews' permission to marry his daughter. His soon-to-be father-in-law had given it.

Now Adrian understood what Stern had been going through while waiting to marry JoJo. More than anything, Adrian couldn't wait for a minister to announce him and Trinity as husband and wife.

"Adrian?"

"Yes, sweetheart?"

"Is something going on with Aidan and one of Pam's sisters?" Trinity asked.

He gazed down at her. "What makes you think that?"

She shrugged and then told him what she'd witnessed earlier.

Adrian nodded. "Yes. He's in love with Jillian and has been for years. No one is supposed to know that he and Jillian once had a secret affair…especially not Pam and Dillon. Aidan and Jillian ended their affair last year."

Trinity stopped walking and raised a brow. "Why?"

He told her the little about the situation that he knew.

"Do you think they will work everything out and get back together?" Trinity asked softly.

"Yes," Adrian said with certainty.

Trinity glanced up at him. "How can you be so sure?"

Adrian stopped walking and wrapped his arms around Trinity. "I can feel his determination, and the only thing I've got to say is that Jillian better watch out. Aidan is coming after her and he's determined to get her back."

Not wanting to dwell on Aidan and his issues, Adrian kissed Trinity once, and planned on doing a whole lot more.

* * * * *

*If you loved Adrian's story,
don't miss his brother Aidan's tale
THE SECRET AFFAIR
September 2014!*

Only from New York Times *bestselling author
Brenda Jackson and Harlequin Desire!*

COMING NEXT MONTH FROM

 HARLEQUIN®

 *Desire*

Available April 1, 2014

#2293 ONE GOOD COWBOY
Diamonds in the Rough • by Catherine Mann
To inherit the family business, CEO Stone McNair must prove he isn't heartless underneath his ruthlessly suave exterior. His trial? Finding homes for rescue dogs. His judge? The ex-fiancée who's heart he broke.

#2294 THE BLACK SHEEP'S INHERITANCE
Dynasties: The Lassiters • by Maureen Child
Suspicious of his late father's nurse when she inherits millions in his father's will, Sage Lassiter is determined to get the truth. Even if he has to seduce it out of her.

#2295 HIS LOVER'S LITTLE SECRET
Billionaires and Babies • by Andrea Laurence
Artist Sabine Hayes fell hard for shipping magnate Gavin Brooks, and when it was over, she found herself pregnant. Now he's come to demand his son—and the passion they've both denied.

#2296 A NOT-SO-INNOCENT SEDUCTION
The Kavanaghs of Silver Glen • by Janice Maynard
The sexy but stoic Liam has headed the Kavanagh family since his reckless father's disappearance two decades ago. But meeting the innocent, carefree Zoe awakens his passions, derailing his sense of duty.

#2297 WANTING WHAT SHE CAN'T HAVE
The Master Vintners • by Yvonne Lindsay
Her best friend's last wish was that Alexis care for her baby—and her husband. So Alexis becomes the nanny, determined to heal this family without falling for the one man she can't have.

#2298 ONCE PREGNANT, TWICE SHY
by Red Garnier
Wealthy Texan Garret Gage promised to protect family friend Kate just as fiercely as her father would have. And he'd been doing just fine, until one night of passion changes everything.

YOU CAN FIND MORE INFORMATION ON UPCOMING HARLEQUIN® TITLES, FREE EXCERPTS AND MORE AT WWW.HARLEQUIN.COM.

HDCNM0314

REQUEST YOUR FREE BOOKS!
2 FREE NOVELS PLUS 2 FREE GIFTS!

HARLEQUIN®

Desire

ALWAYS POWERFUL, PASSIONATE AND PROVOCATIVE

YES! Please send me 2 FREE Harlequin Desire® novels and my 2 FREE gifts (gifts are worth about $10). After receiving them, if I don't wish to receive any more books, I can return the shipping statement marked "cancel." If I don't cancel, I will receive 6 brand-new novels every month and be billed just $4.55 per book in the U.S. or $4.99 per book in Canada. That's a savings of at least 13% off the cover price! It's quite a bargain! Shipping and handling is just 50¢ per book in the U.S. and 75¢ per book in Canada.* I understand that accepting the 2 free books and gifts places me under no obligation to buy anything. I can always return a shipment and cancel at any time. Even if I never buy another book, the two free books and gifts are mine to keep forever.

225/326 HDN F4ZC

Name	(PLEASE PRINT)	

Address		Apt. #

City	State/Prov.	Zip/Postal Code

Signature (if under 18, a parent or guardian must sign)

Mail to the Harlequin® Reader Service:
IN U.S.A.: P.O. Box 1867, Buffalo, NY 14240-1867
IN CANADA: P.O. Box 609, Fort Erie, Ontario L2A 5X3

Want to try two free books from another line?
Call 1-800-873-8635 or visit www.ReaderService.com.

* Terms and prices subject to change without notice. Prices do not include applicable taxes. Sales tax applicable in N.Y. Canadian residents will be charged applicable taxes. Offer not valid in Quebec. This offer is limited to one order per household. Not valid for current subscribers to Harlequin Desire books. All orders subject to credit approval. Credit or debit balances in a customer's account(s) may be offset by any other outstanding balance owed by or to the customer. Please allow 4 to 6 weeks for delivery. Offer available while quantities last.

Your Privacy—The Harlequin® Reader Service is committed to protecting your privacy. Our Privacy Policy is available online at www.ReaderService.com or upon request from the Harlequin Reader Service.

We make a portion of our mailing list available to reputable third parties that offer products we believe may interest you. If you prefer that we not exchange your name with third parties, or if you wish to clarify or modify your communication preferences, please visit us at www.ReaderService.com/consumerschoice or write to us at Harlequin Reader Service Preference Service, P.O. Box 9062, Buffalo, NY 14269. Include your complete name and address.

HD13R

SPECIAL EXCERPT FROM

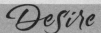

Read on for a sneak peek at
USA TODAY *bestselling author*
Maureen Child's
THE BLACK SHEEP'S INHERITANCE,
the debut novel in Harlequin® Desire's
DYNASTIES: THE LASSITERS series.

*A Wyoming business legend dies and leaves his nurse a
fortune. Now his son wants answers...*

"**C**olleen!"

That deep voice was unmistakable. Colleen had been
close to Sage Lassiter only one time before today. The night
of his sister's rehearsal dinner. From across that crowded
restaurant, she'd felt him watching her. The heat of his gaze
had swamped her, sending ribbons of expectation unfurl-
ing throughout her body. He'd smiled and her stomach had
churned with swarms of butterflies. He'd headed toward
her, and she'd told herself to be calm. Cool. But it hadn't
worked. Nerves had fired, knees weakened.

And just as he had been close enough to her that she
could see the gleam in his eyes, J.D. had had his heart attack
and everything had changed forever.

Sage Lassiter *stalked* across the parking lot toward her.
He was like a man on a mission. He wore dark jeans, boots
and an expensively cut black sport jacket over a long-
sleeved white shirt. His brown hair flew across his forehead
and his blue eyes were narrowed against the wind. In a few
short seconds, he was there. Right in front of her.

She had to tip her head back to meet his gaze and when she did, nerves skated down along her spine.

"I'm so sorry about your father."

A slight frown crossed his face. "Thanks. Look, I wanted to talk to you—"

"You did?" There went her silly heart again, jumping into a gallop.

"Yes. I've got a couple questions…."

Fascination dissolved into truth. Here she was, day-dreaming about a gorgeous man suddenly paying attention to her when the reality was he'd just lost his father. As J.D.'s private nurse, she'd be the first he'd turn to.

"Of course you do." Instinctively, she reached out, laid her hand on his and felt a swift jolt of electricity jump from his body to hers.

His eyes narrowed further and she knew he'd felt it, too.

Shaking his head, he said, "No. I don't have any questions about J.D. You went from nurse to millionaire in a few short months. Actually, *you're* the mystery here."

Read more of
THE BLACK SHEEP'S INHERITANCE,
available April 2014
wherever Harlequin® Desire and ebooks are sold.

Copyright © 2014 by Maureen Child

HDEXP0314

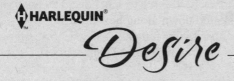

HARLEQUIN®

Desire

ALWAYS POWERFUL, PASSIONATE AND PROVOCATIVE.

ONCE PREGNANT, TWICE SHY
Red Garnier

What's one impulsive night between old friends?

Tied together by tragedy, wealthy Texan tycoon Garret Gage promised to protect family friend Kate just as fiercely as her father would have. And he'd been doing just fine until one night of passion and a secret changes everything.

Look for
ONCE PREGNANT, TWICE SHY
by Red Garnier April 2014 from Harlequin® Desire!

Wherever books and ebooks are sold.

Also by Red Garnier
WRONG MAN, RIGHT KISS

www.Harlequin.com

HD73311

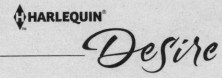

HARLEQUIN®
Desire

ALWAYS POWERFUL, PASSIONATE AND PROVOCATIVE.

HIS LOVER'S LITTLE SECRET
Billionaires and Babies
by Andrea Laurence

She's kept her baby secret for two years...

But even after a chance run-in forces her to confront the father of her son, Sabine Hayes refuses to give in to shipping magnate Gavin Brooks's demands. His power and his wealth won't turn her head this time. But Gavin never stopped wanting the woman who challenged him at every turn. He has a right to claim what's his...and he'll do just about anything to prevent her from getting away from him again.

Look for HIS LOVER'S LITTLE SECRET
by Andrea Laurence April 2014, from Harlequin® Desire!

Don't miss other scandalous titles from the
Billionaires and Babies miniseries,
available now wherever ebooks are sold.

DOUBLE THE TROUBLE by Maureen Child
YULETIDE BABY SURPRISE by Catherine Mann
CLAIMING HIS OWN by Elizabeth Gates
A BILLIONAIRE FOR CHRISTMAS by Janice Maynard
THE NANNY'S SECRET by Elizabeth Lane
SNOWBOUND WITH A BILLIONAIRE by Jules Bennett

HD73308